KEEPER

OF THE

LIGHT

KEEPER OF THE LIGHT

Patricia Curtis Pfitsch

Simon & Schuster Books for Young Readers

SIMON & SCHUSTER BOOKS FOR YOUNG READERS
An imprint of Simon & Schuster Children's Publishing Division
1230 Avenue of the Americas
New York, New York 10020
Text copyright © 1997 by Patricia Curtis Pfitsch
Book design by Anahid Hamparian
The text of this book is set in 14-point Palatino.
Printed and bound in the United States of America
First Edition
10 9 8 7 6 5

Library of Congress Cataloging-in-Publication Data

Pfitsch, Patricia Curtis.
Keeper of the light / by Patricia Curtis Pfitsch.
p   .cm.
Includes bibliographical references.
Summary: After her father's death in 1872, Faith takes over his job as
lighthouse keeper on Lake Superior, until her mother decides to move into town, where
Faith finds herself stifled by the role society expects her to play.
ISBN 0-689-81492-5
[1. Lighthouses—Fiction. 2. Sex role—Fiction. 3. Michigan—Fiction.] I. Title.
PZ7.P448555Ke 1997 [Fic]—dc21 96-39745 CIP AC

To my children,
Holly, Woody, and Jane,
who believed in me from the beginning

Acknowledgments

Someone once told me that it takes two people to make an artist: one to do the art, and the other to take care of everything else. In my case, it takes five. I write, and my family keeps our life together while I'm doing it. Loving thanks to Jack and my kids for supporting and loving me in the bad times as well as the good, and for telling me the truth. Thanks to my parents, Edie and George Curtis, who are always there to help when I need it. I love you.

Thanks to Judi, Sheri, Joan, Stephanie, Suzanne, and Kathy, and to all my cyber-sisters for your wisdom and understanding. And to George and David for your belief in me.

Thanks to the Great Lakes Shipwreck Historical Museum in Whitefish Point, Michigan, for information on lighthouses and Lake Superior Shipwrecks, and to John Flint of the Shore Village Museum, in Rockland, Maine, for information on Fresnel lenses. Many thanks to Maura Otis, the librarian in Gays Mills, Wisconsin, for her cheerful willingness to look for whatever information I need, no matter how obscure. For the sake of my story, I've taken some liberties with the geography of the upper peninsula of Michigan. Though Munising is a real town, the Port Henry Lighthouse and Token Creek are imaginary places. No character in this book bears any intentional resemblance to any real person, living or dead.

one

The edge of the world. Faith squinted, searching for that pencil-thin line far off the Lake Superior shore where flat gray sky met flat gray water. She dug her toes into the cold beach and shook sand from the folds of her skirts. It had been gray since morning. The wind carried the musty scent of rain, and the clouds hung so low they almost touched the black tip of the pointed lighthouse roof.

"Do you see anything?" Willy asked, wiping his hands on his knickers. Her brother was supposed to be helping Faith polish the brass lanterns, but he was trying to tame gulls, instead.

"No," Faith answered. She listened to the rising wind and watched as Willy squatted on the stretch of sand beach between the lighthouse and the keeper's house. He held out a crust of bread, keeping his hand still as a stone. A gull landed and began to pace closer and closer. Then, with a quick stab, the bird grabbed the crust and flew off a few feet with his prize.

"Better hurry," Faith said, wiping the last of the soot from her lantern chimney. "It'll storm soon." The familiar mixture of excitement and fear rose in her, and she shivered.

"I know," Willy said, pointing. "Look at the birds."

Faith watched the gulls swooping low over the white foam waves. "Papa said he could tell how bad a storm

1

would be by the way the gulls flew," she said.

"He could?" Willy turned his big questioning eyes from the birds to Faith. "Can you?" he asked. "Will it be bad tonight?"

She shook her head, wishing her father *had* explained it. But he never did, and now it was too late. It had been over five months since he'd drowned, and Faith had kept the lighthouse beacon burning every night since then on her own. She hadn't missed even one hour of darkness. She had made a promise, and she meant to keep it.

"You'd better get your work done before it starts to rain. Mama will be furious if you get wet." She tossed a cloth to Willy, who plopped down on the flat-topped boulder they used as both bench and worktable.

He made a face at her and pulled the other lantern to him. "She treats me like a baby," he grumbled, "and she lets you do anything you want."

"She just doesn't want you to get sick again," Faith said. "And she *doesn't* let me do everything I want."

Willy scrubbed the glass in silence while the wind blew wisps of his blond hair into his eyes. Then, "She told me we're going to stay in town this winter after the locks close. She said it would be better for me." He stopped polishing.

"I know," Faith said, frowning. When she was younger, Mama used to take them to visit her family every year, but since Grandmother Burleigh had died, their trips to Token Creek had been rare and quickly over. Faith was glad; there were too many rules in town.

Her mother used to give her the same lecture each time the steamer pulled up to the dock at Token Creek. "Now remember," she'd say, "Grandmother believes that children should be seen and not heard, Faith. You must learn to curb your tongue. And no running in the house. Grandmother expects you to be a lady."

"Willy runs in the house."

"Willy is a boy, and younger than you." Her mother would straighten Willy's sailor jacket and retie Faith's hair ribbons.

"Can we go outside, then?" Faith had always asked.

"We'll see," her mother would answer. "Perhaps we can walk in the park in the evenings."

But walking slowly down the grassy paths of the park in the town square, standing stiff and quiet while Mother spoke with strange women, that wasn't what Faith had in mind. She was sure she would go mad if she had to spend all winter pretending to be a lady.

Faith looked at Willy as he cleaned his lantern. "Mama said we'll get to go to a real school," he said. He didn't look all that happy about it.

"You'll do fine." Faith answered his worried look. "You're the friendly one, remember?" She wasn't so sure about herself. She couldn't imagine being cooped up in a room for hours with thirty other children. All those eyes looking at her! Her hands shook just thinking about it.

"Being here all winter wouldn't be the same, anyway," Willy said, too loud. He took a sudden interest in one black smudge on the lantern glass. A tear trickled down his cheek, but he wiped it away with the polishing cloth.

Faith pretended not to see. She bit her lip and looked at the lighthouse perched out on the rocks with the lake all around it, like a slender white finger pointing toward heaven. The red brick keeper's house was nestled into the side of the pink sandstone bluff behind her, with the gray clapboard outbuildings clustered around it like chicks around a hen. The buildings looked tiny in comparison with the tall lighthouse. Faith had lived there since she was four, and except for one long winter in town she preferred not to think about, they'd stayed at the lighthouse even after the lake froze and shipping stopped for the winter. This would be the first winter Willy had ever spent away from the lighthouse. It would be the first winter either of them had spent without their father.

No more tramping through the snowy woods, checking the traps. No more evenings by the fire, listening while Willy practiced reading and she worked the arithmetic problems her mother set for her. No more geography lessons at the dining room table with the huge yellowed map of the world spread out in front of them.

"Anyway, December is months away," she said, trying to sound cheerful. "And we'll come back in the spring."

"Not if they find a new keeper," Willy pointed out. His pale face looked almost white in the dim afternoon light.

Faith sat down beside him on the boulder. "They haven't found one yet," she said. "I've been watching the mail. Mama's had lots of letters from her friends in Token Creek, but not even one with the Lighthouse Board's return address." Maybe her wish would come true after all, she thought for the thousandth time. Maybe they wouldn't find a new keeper.

She closed her eyes and listened to the low thunder of the waves on the beach. In her mind she saw her father in his dark blue keeper's uniform, arms outstretched to the lake and the gulls. For an instant she thought she heard him laugh. Her eyes blinked open, and her heart thumped loud in her ears.

But the beach was empty. She kicked at the sand. He wasn't going to come back, she told herself. Ever. "Bring your lantern when you're done," she instructed Willy. "I'm going to light the beacon." She headed for the house.

"Storm's coming, Mama," she called, banging the door behind her as she came into the kitchen. The sweet smell of cooking onions made her mouth water.

4

"Another one?" Her mother used a corner of her apron to slide the hot skillet to the back of the big black cookstove. "It seems we can't even see the last of one storm before another blows in."

Faith heard her sigh. Even before Papa died her mother had not shared their love for stormy weather. And now she hated it. "Where's Willy?" she said.

"He's polishing his lantern. He'll come in a minute," Faith answered, tired of the now familiar anxiety in her mother's voice. "Stop worrying so much."

Her mother's shoulders stiffened. "Don't talk back, Faith. It's dangerous for your brother to be out in a storm."

"I wasn't talking back." Faith put the lantern down on the bare wooden worktable. "I was just trying to tell you there isn't any danger yet."

Her mother interrupted her. "You must learn to show respect for your elders."

"Yes, ma'am," Faith answered, gritting her teeth. She went to the window, pushed back the yellow curtains, and looked out at the stark and empty beach, at the clean white sand and the dark water streaked with white foam waves. The purple-gray clouds were building up into huge fantastic shapes. "Mama?" She put her finger on the cold glass. "Can't you see how beautiful the lake is?"

But her mother wouldn't even look out the window. She rubbed her arms with her hands. "It swallows up everything around it," she muttered. "It's angry and dangerous."

"We'll be safe enough," Faith answered. "The sailors are the ones in danger."

"No." Her mother spun around. "That's what your father thought, and he died for it. I will not lose you, as well."

"You used to like it," Faith said, clenching her fists.

5

"When Papa was alive you loved the lake."

"I never loved it," she answered, staring out at the water.

Faith wanted to shake her. "Don't you remember how you and Papa walked on the beach? You even liked wading." She was almost as tall as her mother, and now she stood in front of her, eye to eye. "It hasn't been that long, Mother. How could you forget?"

They stared at each other for a long moment. Then her mother let her hands drop to her sides. "You have no idea how I really felt," she said. She shoved a piece of kindling into the firebox on the stove and let the heavy lid fall back with a hollow clang.

Faith could stand it no longer. She grabbed up the tin of thick fish oil and set it on the back of the stove to warm. She knew better than anyone that it had to be thin and watery before it could burn properly in the lighthouse lamps. "I'm going to polish the lens," she said. She picked up a soft cotton cloth from the pile they kept folded on the dresser by the door and slipped her feet into her father's old galoshes.

She wrapped herself in a heavy wool cloak just as Willy came bursting through the door. "The storm's coming fast," he cried, handing Faith the lantern.

"Thanks," she shouted over the roar of the wind. "You can bring me the oil when it's warmed through."

"Take it now." Her mother's voice stopped them both. "I will not have him out on the walkway in this weather."

Faith turned in the doorway. "Then I'll come back for it," she snapped. If the oil wasn't warm enough, it would clog in the mechanism and the light would go out. She'd made that mistake once. She would never make it again. She banged the door closed, and headed for the lighthouse.

two

They didn't live on an island, but they might as well have. That was one of the things Faith liked about it. On the map, it looked like the white lighthouse was only a few short miles down the beach from Token Creek. But that was the map. The truth was that the rough path was usually covered with water, and scrambling along the crumbling sandstone bluffs was too dangerous. The only safe way to get to the lighthouse grounds from town was by boat.

The tower itself had been built at the end of a line of half-submerged boulders that extended out into the lake; a narrow wooden walkway with a railing on either side led to it. The walkway was raised a few feet above the level of the lake, and it always gave Faith the feeling she was walking right on top of the water. Especially on days like this, when it boiled up, and she had to wade through the waves washing over the planks. Faith held tight to the railings for balance, leaned into the wind, and lifted her feet high. It was almost like a wrestling match. "I'm winning," she shouted to the wind.

She reached the lighthouse door, pulled it open, and slipped inside. She could hear the wind whistling around the walls, crying as if it were sad to find itself still outside. She threw back her hood and began to climb the eighty-six steps to the light.

It was a fourth-order Fresnel lens, small for a lighthouse

lens, but more than half as tall as Faith was, herself. When the sun touched the lens, the multifacets of the glass bathed the tower room in a shower of tiny rainbows. Even on as gray a day as this, the glass reflected light like a mirror, making the tower room by far the brightest spot on the grounds.

Faith touched the cool smooth face of the glass with the tip of her finger and quickly wiped the spot with her cloth. There could be no smudges to dim the power of the lens. She turned toward the lake. When she looked out the tower windows, she felt like a gull soaring almost into the clouds. If her mother would only come up here more often, Faith thought, maybe then she'd feel differently about the lighthouse. She twisted the polishing cloth between her fingers.

Once she had thought her mother was the strongest person in the world. She had heard her father tell the story so often, she knew it by heart. Her mother, daughter of the wealthiest lawyer in Token Creek, had gone against the wishes of her whole family to marry Robert Sutton, the son of an itinerant logger and a barmaid. Next to that kind of defiance, Faith thought, facing the lake in a storm was simple.

She looked out at the angry waves. The lake was never still. Even on calm days the emerald green water was flecked with glints of sunlight sparkling off the restless ripples. Today, the lake was a boiling cauldron. The rolling waves crashed together and pounded the line of rocks, sending fountains of cold spray twenty feet into the air.

They didn't call it "The Graveyard" for nothing, Faith thought. Her father's wasn't the only life it had claimed. That was why her mother feared it so. She leaned on the heavy brass railing that ran around the edges of the room. But how could her mother hate something her father had loved so much? She remembered the warmth of the sand between her shoulder blades when he'd made them all lie down on the beach to watch the gulls. And he'd known every rock they'd brought him. Faith had thought he'd invented the names, until he'd shown her how to look them up in the big black book of minerals he'd kept on the shelf in the parlor.

Faith sighed, wondering what had happened to the book. She hadn't seen it since last spring. She wrapped the rag around her fingers and went over the smooth facets of the lens, removing every smudge of grease and soot. Even a dust speck might dim the power of the light, might mean the difference between life and death for the sailors on the water.

As she rubbed the glass, her anger melted away. Somehow her father was still here in the lighthouse. Faith could feel his eyes watching her. His voice echoed in her ears, repeating each instruction, helping to be sure she made no mistakes. She remembered the touch of his hands guiding hers, showing her just how to polish the lens without scratching it. "Now watch carefully," he'd say, working the lock mechanism and opening the glass door of the lens to reveal the oil lamp inside. "This is the heart of the lighthouse." Night after night she had watched as he trimmed the wicks and lit each one with a touch from the candle.

When she was nine he'd allowed her to light the lamp all by herself. "You'll be keeper someday," he'd said, grabbing her up in a bear hug that almost knocked the breath out of her.

Faith let her breath out in a rush, unaware till then that she'd been holding it. Now she *was* keeper, she thought, and the lighthouse was all she had left of her father.

Full dark had come by the time she ran back through the rain to the house, fetched the bucket of warm oil, filled the reservoir, lit the lamp, and returned to the house. She stopped with her hand on the latch to look back at the tower; the beam of light shone out into the blackness, firm and strong as a glowing bar of iron. It blinked, off again on again, in the familiar heartbeat that identified this as the Port Henry Light. Its bright throbbing lit her bedroom the whole night through; if ever it failed, the sudden darkness woke her as surely as if a firecracker had exploded by her ear.

"Faith's here." Willy's voice sang out as the wind blew her into the house. "We're having potato soup," he said, prancing around the kitchen, which was lit now with the mellow glow of the kerosene lamp on the table. He stopped to touch the fabric of her cloak with his hand. "Is it raining yet?"

She nodded and flicked a few drops at him from her wet fingers. "Hard rain," she said. "Like needles."

"Can I start the foghorn?" Willy planted himself in front of her.

"If we need it," Faith answered, "and if Mama says you may." She kicked off the wet galoshes and shook out her cloak.

Willy's twinkling eyes suddenly lost some of their gleam. "She won't," he said, turning around. "She never lets me do anything. Not since Papa . . ."

"That's enough." Faith looked up at the sound to see her mother's slender figure silhouetted in the kitchen doorway. "Supper is ready," she said, moving into the room. Her face was pale, but there was a spot of color high up on each cheekbone.

Faith and Willy exchanged a glance and sat down at the formal dining table. They used to crowd around the kitchen worktable to eat, poking each other and giggling. Her father had been the worst teaser of them all, but Faith remembered how her mother had sometimes laughed as hard as Willy at his antics. Now her mother always spread a lace cloth on the dining table and set it carefully for meals.

Faith cut the cornbread into fat squares. Her mother dished out three steaming bowls of soup, and then picked up her spoon, the signal that they could all begin to eat. But then she put it down again. "Go ahead," she said, nodding to Faith and Willy. "You eat. I have something to say."

In the silence Faith could hear the wind moaning through the pines on the bluff, and her thoughts went automatically to the light. Had it gone out? Was there a ship off the coast? She half rose in her seat, but stopped when her mother pulled a folded sheet of paper from her pocket and smoothed it out on the table. It was a letter.

"This came in last week's mail packet," her mother said. "It's from Mr. Chesterfield. He says the board has appointed a new keeper."

Faith's hand froze halfway to her mouth with a spoonful of soup. She let the spoon bang down into her bowl, splashing a bit of potato onto the tablecloth.

Her mother frowned at her and began to read the letter. "It's dated August 1, 1872," she said. "'Dear Mrs. Sutton. We of the Lighthouse Board realize the hardship you've been under these past months since the death of your husband. Please accept our sincere apologies. We have finally found a new keeper, a young man who will be able to keep the light burning.'"

"But we HAVE kept the light burning," Faith burst out.

"Hush," her mother said. She went on reading. "'On August twentieth Nathaniel Kent, the new keeper, will be arriving at the lighthouse. Please make a complete inventory of all supplies on hand for his use. It will also be necessary to show him the workings of the beacon, as this is his first post as keeper. We have procured a house on Water

Street in town for your use after you vacate the light-house—you may live here until you make more satisfactory arrangements. Again, our most humble apologies for our tardiness in this matter. We thank you for your good work in the absence of a keeper. Sincerely, Mr. Harlan Chesterfield for the Lighthouse Board.'"

Faith pounded her fist on the table. "I *am* the keeper," she wailed. "The light hasn't gone out once!" She put her hand on her mother's arm. "Tell them we don't want to leave."

Her mother extracted her arm from Faith's grip. "I wrote to Harlan Chesterfield myself," she said. She drew a ragged breath. "I can't live here anymore. When your father was alive it was bearable, but now I need people around."

"We won't have any money," Faith argued. "We'll lose the keeper's salary if we move to town."

Her mother shook her head. "I have an inheritance," she said quietly. "Some land your grandfather owned near Munising. By the terms of his will, if your father died or if we left the lighthouse, it would come to me." She looked at Willy and back to Faith. "I've already arranged to sell it to the lumber company, and with the money from the sale, we will do quite well."

She gave Faith's shoulder a squeeze. "You need to go to school with other girls your age," she said. "And if we lived in town we could go to a concert once in a while. There's a chamber music society. I could play my flute."

Faith watched her mother. She was looking off into some distance Faith couldn't see, hearing some music Faith couldn't hear. "Mama," she cried, "I don't want to live in town."

"How do you know?" Faith's mother folded the letter and slipped it back into her pocket. "You've hardly ever been to town."

Faith jumped up, nearly knocking her chair to the floor. "What about that winter we lived with Uncle Joseph?" she said. "Don't you remember how horrible the cousins were?" She shut her mouth on the other memory, the one of her father and her grandfather yelling at each other every night after dinner.

Faith's mother laughed. "That was a long time ago," she said. "Your cousins wouldn't tease you now—they're all grown up. You'd have fun with them."

"I don't want to know the other girls. I just want to live here and keep the light burning like Papa told us to!" Faith reached out to take her mother's hand.

"Faith!" Her mother drew back. "You're sounding like Willy! You're not a child any longer. You're almost a grown woman, and you must take on the responsibilities of a grown woman."

Faith jerked her head up, flicking her hair back over her shoulder with one hand. "But not the responsibilities of a grown man," she said. "Is that it?" She flung her napkin down on the table and clamped her mouth shut. She would not say another word.

three

When Faith arose at three to wind the clockworks and keep the oil flowing into the burner until dawn, her mother was waiting. "Be careful," she said, helping Faith into the cloak she'd kept warm near the stove. "It's a wild night."

"I will, Mama," she answered, taking the lantern her mother held out to her.

In the flickering light, her mother's eyes were worried. "I'll be glad when we're safely in town," she said. "This is no job for a young girl."

"Perhaps not," Faith snapped. "But it suits me just the same."

Her mother's mouth folded down into a thin line. It was best, Faith knew, not to argue when her mother looked like that. "Be careful," her father used to warn them. "Don't beard the lion in her den." But his twinkling eyes could often draw a smile from her mother even then.

"We're just different, Mama," she said, wishing she had even a little of the same effect on her mother's moods. But it was only fragile little Willy who could make her laugh now.

Her mother sighed. "Not so different as you might think," she said, her mouth softening. She reached out to touch Faith's cheek. She looked as if she might say something more, but then only shook her head and, opening the door, let Faith out into the storm.

Her mother was right about one thing: The night *was* wild. Faith could feel her spirits lifting with the power of the wind. *This* was a fight she had some chance of winning. The wind howled and whipped her cloak straight out behind her; it blew rain hard as sand against her skin. She closed her eyes, leaned into the force of the gale, and struggled closer to the lighthouse. Even though she wasn't frightened, she could hear her own gasping breath as if it were coming from someone else.

Once on the walkway she hooked the lantern over her arm and grabbed tight to the railing with both hands. Hand over hand she pulled herself forward, sliding her feet through the churning water; it would be easier coming home with the wind at her back.

And then, suddenly, there was no longer a railing. She reached forward for the next step and clutched at nothing. She choked off a cry, and her heart pounded in her throat. Caught off balance, she fell forward, but she flung her arm behind her and grabbed the rail on the other side. Her feet scrambled for purchase on the slippery boards, and the lantern handle bit into her arm. Finally she pulled herself to a standing position and lifted the lamp.

Its beam couldn't penetrate the blackness, but in a sudden flash of lightning she saw what had happened. The wooden rail on one side of the walkway had broken in two; the ends were swinging wildly in the wind. It was lucky she hadn't been struck as they washed back and forth with each pounding wave. A low grumble of thunder made an ominous echo to her thought.

But the rail on this side held. Faith took a breath and then slowly, feeling her way more carefully, she moved forward again toward the lighthouse. Her wet cloak and skirt were heavier than ever, but finally the round brass knob of the lighthouse door was in her hands. She turned it, pulled the door open, and slipped inside.

As soon as she was out of the weather, her legs gave way and she sat on the bottom step to rest while she recovered her breath. Then, fearing her passage had taken longer than usual, she jumped up. She hung her soaking cloak on a hook by the door and took the steps two at a time to the top.

The light was still burning. She wound the clockworks and swiped with a rag at some smudges of smoke on the lens. Then she crossed to the window and, placing her hands on either side of her eyes to block out the light, she pressed against the glass and looked out.

She couldn't see anything in the black pouring rain, nothing but glimmers of white as the waves hit the rocks and splashed skyward. Then another flash of lightning lit the lake, and she saw it was empty of the tall-masted schooners with their white sails. She listened to the long roll of thunder and then began the journey back to the house.

She would say nothing of the broken rail, she decided. If her mother knew the truth, she'd never let Faith back out on the walkway, and there were still ten days until the new keeper arrived. The break could be repaired as soon as the storm let up. She would keep the beacon lit until the keeper came. She *would.*

The storm washed the sky clean of clouds, and Faith was out before breakfast the next morning, looking at the break in the railing. The air was crisp. The breeze blowing through the pines on the bluff sounded like a rushing river. She could smell autumn on the wind, but the sand was warm under her feet, and the lake was calm and blue, a perfect mirror of the sky.

"Faith," her mother called out. "It's time to eat."

Faith could see her standing in the doorway, shielding her eyes from the bright morning sun. "Go ahead and start, Mama," she called back. "I'll be there in a minute." She stepped out onto the walkway. There was a bulge in the plank right at the place where the railing had broken.

"Faith!" Now her mother had both hands on her hips. "We sit down all together or not at all."

Faith sighed, remembering how on fine days they used to bring their breakfast outside and eat on the beach when Papa was alive. "I'm coming, Mama," she called back.

"What were you looking at?" her mother asked when they were all three sitting at the table.

"The storm did some damage to the walkway; that's all," Faith said. Quickly she began eating her oatmeal, knowing her mother would never make her talk with her mouth full.

But it seemed her mother was too busy with her own plans to give a thought to things like a broken walkway. "We must start packing today," she said. "I want both of you to go through your clothes. Willy, you are to try on everything."

"Everything, Mama?" His face took on an air of desperation.

"Well, at least everything you don't wear all the time. I'll help you." She turned to Faith, tapping her finger on the table. "I don't see any reason for taking those old work skirts you wear around here," she said.

Faith stopped eating. "I think I'll take them, Mama," she said. She would not leave her favorite clothes here to be turned into rags for the new keeper.

Her mother picked up her spoon, ate a few bites of oatmeal, and then looked at Faith. "You will wear your nice things when you're in town, won't you?" she said. There was a hint of something in her eyes, an almost pleading look that suddenly made Faith want to cry. Who was this woman her mother was turning into? She had never before worried about Faith's clothes.

"Mama, you know how I hate my fancy dresses," she said. "I can't *do* anything when I'm wearing them. And they lace so tight, I can hardly breathe."

Her mother sighed. "You won't have physical labor to do in town, Faith," she said, exaggerated patience in the carefully pronounced words. "You'll be studying and meeting for tea with your friends. You have a nice voice; we'll enroll you for singing lessons. You'll have no need for the kind of clothes you've been wearing."

Faith scraped up the last bites of oatmeal in her bowl and stood. "You don't understand," she said, trying to keep her voice calm. "I can't sit around all day and have tea. I have to be doing something important."

Her mother put down her napkin and rose to face Faith. "If you think," she began, but her voice was shaking. She stopped and took a deep breath. "Education is one of the most important things a woman can do for herself," she said. "If you think I will let you grow up like a country bumpkin, with no advantages, you can just think again." Her eyes flashed, and her voice was steady.

Faith clenched her fists. "I'm educated, Mama," she said, trying to keep her own voice even. "I know how to read and figure. I know geography and history. You taught me yourself. Why was that good enough when Papa was alive, but not good enough now? Why am I a country bumpkin all of a sudden?" She swallowed back the tears she could feel swimming behind her eyes. Her mother would *not* see her cry. "May I be excused now? I need to fix the walkway."

four

Faith marched down the beach to the walkway, pounding her feet in the sand with each step. "Who cares what she thinks," Faith mumbled. Shaking away tears, she examined the damage. The waves must have washed a huge rock over the walkway in the storm; there were two badly cracked planks, and one side of the railing was broken clear in two. Faith held on to the intact section of rail and shuddered. What would have happened if both railings had broken?

"Stop thinking of the danger," she told herself sternly. Her father had said the same thing to her mother the night the *Alice Rutherford* cracked up on the rocks. The words echoed in her ears, and she saw the image of her mother as she clutched her father's arm, begging him not to launch the lifeboat. It was the last time they'd seen him alive.

But he was right. Faith examined the jagged ends of the railing. If you thought of the danger, you'd leave the lighthouse and never come back. Like her mother, she thought.

The storehouse where they kept the firewood for the stove and extra pieces of railing and planks had only one window. It was dust and water spotted; Faith stood in the doorway, letting her eyes adjust to the dimness. There was plenty of wood: piles of wide planks longer than Faith was tall, small pieces stacked like firewood, and an assortment of boards of various sizes. Faith picked up one of the longest planks and stood it on end to examine it.

"Can I help?" Willy came bursting into the storeroom, tripped over a pile of wood, and fell to his hands and knees in the dirt at Faith's feet.

"Not like that," she said. She hauled him up by one arm and dusted off his knickers. "Besides, I thought you had to try on clothes."

"Mama's fed up with me," Willy explained, grinning. "I won't hold still." He put his hand on the board Faith had leaned against the wall. "Please?"

"All right." Faith tousled her brother's curly hair and rested her palm against his forehead. "But don't get too tired." His eyes were bright, like they'd been when he was sick.

"I don't have a fever," Willy retorted, pulling away from her. "I'm just fine."

"I know," Faith said, thinking his face still looked thin and drawn. She wondered if he would ever recover fully from the pneumonia. He'd gotten soaked and chilled when they were all out looking for Papa, and he'd almost died, too.

"What are we doing?" he asked.

"Fixing the walkway. It got broken in the storm."

"With you on it?" Willy's eyes were wide and shining. "Were you scared?"

"I didn't say I was on it, did I, Mr. Nosy?" Faith picked up one end of the board. "Now help me carry this out into the light."

Willy picked up the other end, and together they dragged the board out of the storehouse and dropped it in the sandy soil of the lighthouse yard. Mama had struggled to get real grass to grow, but finally she'd given up and let the tough, stringy dune grass come up, instead. It was sparse and scattered, but Faith thought that slowly it would fill in all the bare patches. She looked out at the lake. Now they wouldn't be here to see it happen.

She paced the length of the board, counting her steps. "I don't think that's going to be long enough," she said.

Willy flopped down on the board. "It's long enough for me," he said.

Faith looked at him. "Long enough to replace the broken plank," she said. "Come on, Willy. If you want to help, help!"

They carried the board down to the walkway and lined it up on top of the broken plank. It covered the crack, but it was a good two feet short of the crosspiece that held the planks in place.

Faith stood on the board and looked across the water to the lighthouse.

"Now what?" asked Willy.

"I think we should nail this one down on top of the broken one," Faith answered, thinking out loud. "It would be stronger if we could replace the broken plank with an unbroken one, but we can't, so this will have to do. It won't last the winter, but at least it'll be better than nothing."

"I'll help. I'm good at nailing."

Faith laughed at him. "You are, that's a fact," she said.

Willy ran for the hammer and nails and began his job immediately. Faith dragged another board to the walkway to cover the other cracked plank.

"When you're done with that one," she said, aligning the two planks perfectly, "you can nail this one if you're not too tired."

"Right," Willy said. He wiped his sweaty forehead with his sleeve.

Faith had also brought two of the smaller pieces and some stout rope to fix the railing. When she began winding the rope around the sticks, Willy stopped his pounding.

"What kind of a knot is that?" he asked, putting his finger on the rope.

"One Papa taught me," Faith said. "I can't remember the name of it. We could use a few more to hold the railing together. Do you want to learn it?"

Willy nodded.

"All right then, watch carefully," she said. "First, make a loop around the wood." As she took the end of the rope in her hand, she could almost hear her father's voice saying the very same words; she could see his hands, rough and callused, holding the rope.

Willy looked up at her. "I remember when you learned knots," he said, seeming to read her mind. "You sat beside Papa on the rocks over there." He pointed to the boulders where yesterday they'd sat to polish the lantern.

"That's right," she said, swallowing hard.

"So now you show me." Willy tugged at the rope.

She took a deep breath and let it out. Then she threaded the end of the rope in and out through the loop, making a neat figure-eight shape, and pulled it tight. "See?" She pointed with her finger. "It goes under here and then over."

"Let me try it," Willy said. He held out his hand for the rope, and when she handed it to him, he made a loop and quickly wove the end through it. "Like that?" he said, pulling it tight.

The knot was uneven, but it would hold. "You did it!" she said.

"As good as Papa?" Willy asked.

"Well, no." Faith touched the tip of his nose with the end of the rope. "Not that good. But it's only your first one. Keep on practicing till you run out of rope."

Willy concentrated on the knots. Faith knelt by the planks and picked up the hammer to finish nailing the wood.

And then she heard a sound. A high, clear note filled the

air around them before fading away. Then another note, this time a little lower, and then a ripple of music like a bird's song.

Willy looked up from his rope work. "What's that?"

It had been so long since she'd heard the sound, that at first Faith wasn't sure herself what it was. And when she remembered, she knew the memory came from a time before they'd moved to the lighthouse. "That's Mama playing her flute," Faith answered.

Willy shook his head. "I want to go watch her," he said.

Faith put out a hand. "No," she said. "Let her be. You have to finish the knots."

Willy went back to the railing, and Faith sat with the hammer in her lap, listening to the crystal sound of the flute climbing up and up and then swooping down like a gull diving toward the water. Why had she waited so long to play it? Faith wondered. Listening took her breath away, made her heart ache so, she wanted to scream. Yet when the haunting melody faded away, she wanted it back again.

"Now can I go see her?" Willy said when it was clear there would be no more song. "I've done all my knots."

Faith nodded. He took off, his steps rattling the planks on the walkway. Faith raised the hammer to begin pounding the nails, but then she laid it down again. She could not foul the air with tuneless pounding. At least not for a while.

five

Faith usually looked forward to the steamer coming, bringing supplies, the mail, and a few visitors in the summer. This time it brought the new keeper. Faith heard the sound of the engine and looked out the lighthouse window in time to see it, squat and ugly, chugging up to the landing as if nothing short of a tidal wave could stop it.

She was watching when the new keeper came on deck. He carried one large bag and one small one, and a sailor followed him with a spindly legged table and a kerosene lamp, presumably the keeper's own additions to the furniture provided by the Lighthouse Board.

He stood at the rail surveying the grounds. She saw him look at the house and the outbuildings. He glanced to the lighthouse itself, and then down to the ramp as he took his first steps off the steamer. He was tall, but thin—her father's uniform would hang on him. She wondered whether the Lighthouse Board would alter it or order him up another one.

Her mother stood on the shore. Faith stepped back from the glass when she saw her mother look up to the lighthouse tower windows. She wanted to stay up in the tower, surrounded by the emptiness of the lake forever, but she knew she was expected below. She gritted her teeth and started down the steps.

"Faith, this is Nathaniel Kent, the new keeper." Her

mother's mouth smiled, but Faith saw the warning in her eyes and knew that if she were anything less than civil, there would be trouble.

Nathaniel Kent held out his hand. Faith took it, but when she looked up at him she almost gasped out loud. He was so young! He couldn't be more than three or four years older than Faith herself. So why couldn't they have just hired her, instead? At least they'd have someone with experience.

She tried not to let her thoughts show in her face, but she could see puzzlement in the keeper's light blue eyes. "Mr. Kent," she said. "Welcome to Port Henry Lighthouse."

"Thank you, Miss Sutton." He nodded. "I'm looking forward to being here, and I'm sure you're just as anxious to move back to civilization."

Faith turned away. "Yes. Perhaps we'd better get started. I'll show you the storehouse first. I'm afraid we're a bit low on supplies. Did Mr. Chesterfield mention anything about a shipment before you left?"

But the keeper was staring at her. "Pardon me," Faith said. "Is there anything wrong?"

"I'm perfectly willing to wait for your father," Nathaniel Kent said. "There's no need to hurry on my account."

Her mother's face went white.

"We'd have to wait a long time for my father," Faith replied. "He was drowned last spring when the *Alice Rutherford* went down."

"But . . . ," Nathaniel Kent stopped and looked from Faith's mother to Faith. His cheeks reddened. "I'm sorry. I understood there was a keeper on the grounds to train me." He looked at the steamer as if he wanted to run back on board.

"I'm the keeper," Faith said. It felt good to say it out loud.

His eyes went wide. "You? But you're only a girl."

Faith bit her lip, and her mother answered for her. "Nevertheless, Mr. Kent," she said, and her voice was smooth and low, "Faith has been acting keeper since my husband . . . passed away. She will be the best one to show you your duties."

Faith looked at her mother, surprised at the pride in her voice.

But Nathaniel Kent put his bag down on a flat rock and rolled up his sleeves. "Well, then," he said. "Let's get busy. What was the board thinking of, leaving you here alone with no man to care for you?" He shook his head, and the expression he turned on them was full of sympathy.

That was the last straw. Faith swung around. "Mr. Kent," she said, trying to keep her voice steady. "The Lighthouse Board was probably thinking that a new keeper wasn't needed. Though we miss my father terribly, we have managed quite well. The light has been lit every night. Let's hope you can do likewise."

Nathaniel Kent raised one eyebrow. "Well, Miss Sutton, if that's a challenge, I accept. Will you show me the storehouse?"

It took most of the day to show the keeper his duties. She took him through the sheds, helped him launch the lifeboat, and showed him exactly where to store all the supplies. Each time they came out of a building, the sun was lower in the sky. Her last day was passing, and Faith was forced to spend it instructing an inexperienced keeper.

He listened closely, she had to give him that. But there were times when the slight wrinkle between his brows made her think not all she was saying was registering. She began to wish she'd written everything down.

"The Lighthouse Board will probably expect you to put up your own wood supply," she said, showing him the collection of axes and saws in the storage shed. "You'll receive regular deliveries of staples by steamer, and the garden is just to the south of the house." She looked at him doubtfully. "I don't suppose you'll be canning your own vegetables."

Somehow the keeper's smile made her want to grit her teeth. "My mother offered to keep me supplied with canned goods," he said. "So don't worry your head about that."

Faith refrained from mentioning that she wasn't at all worried about it.

"How often do they send the oil for the beacon?" he asked, resting his hand on the big barrel in the oil shed.

"You'll have to order it," Faith answered. "It takes about three weeks to receive a shipment from town. We try to get the whole year's supply at once, but often the order is short." What if he forgot to order more in time, and the light went out for lack of oil? Her stomach churned at the thought.

"And in cool weather the oil must be warmed so it flows easily into the wicks," she added, looking away from him. She knew this last fact only too well. It was the one thing she could never let herself forget. "If the oil is sluggish, the light will go out."

He nodded. "Maybe you'd better show me how to light it," he said, his eyes straying to the lighthouse windows towering above them.

Faith raised her eyes to the tiny black roof pointing toward the sky. She couldn't put it off any longer. "Yes," she said. She led him to the beach. "We reach the lighthouse by means of the walkway." She pointed out the broken railing and the heavy ship's rope holding it together. "There was an accident last week. I've put in a request for a new railing, but I've gotten no response yet. Perhaps you'll have better luck."

Nathaniel Kent examined Willy's knots. "How long was the light out of commission?" he asked.

It was Faith's turn to stare. "It was never out of commission," she said.

He looked across to the lighthouse and then back at her. "But how did you cross to the lighthouse with no railing and no pathway?" He gestured to the half-submerged rocks below.

"You don't seem to understand, Mr. Kent," Faith began, trying to be patient. "It's the sworn duty of the keeper to keep the lamp lit." She frowned. "If you don't think you can handle the job, you should take the steamer back to Token Creek and inform Mr. Chesterfield. It will be no dishonor. Simply explain they failed to make clear the dangers associated with the job." She looked at him, feeling hope grow in her heart like a flower. Maybe he'd go back.

Instead he shrugged and raised his eyes to hers. "Surely the job couldn't be that dangerous, Miss Sutton," he said, "if a pretty young girl such as yourself could do it." He smiled at her, and his blue eyes twinkled in the afternoon sunlight.

Faith gripped the railing so hard, her fingers turned white. "If you choose to minimize the dangers of the job," she said, not bothering to try to conceal her anger, "that's up to you. But let me remind you that only five months ago my father drowned carrying out the job you're about to take on. Please follow me."

She turned from the water; every step rattled the planks as she walked to the lighthouse. She didn't look behind to see if he was following. She grabbed the heavy brass doorknob and flung the door open.

At the same time, Nathaniel Kent stepped forward, and the door hit him full force, knocking him against the railing. He floundered for his footing, and without thinking, Faith grabbed his arm, steadying him.

"Thank you," he said when he was standing solidly on the walkway again. He ran a hand through his sandy hair and looked at her.

"I'm sorry," she said. "I didn't mean to open the door so fast."

He raised one eyebrow, obviously skeptical. He swung the door gently back and forth with one hand, as if testing its weight.

Faith felt herself blushing. "I didn't!" she protested. "And I didn't know you were going to lean forward like that."

"I thought you might need help," he said. "It's heavy enough."

Faith sighed. "Mr. Kent, I've assisted my father in his duties since I was five years old. For the past five months I've been the keeper."

"And you'd rather keep on doing it," he added.

Faith was standing in the doorway of the tower; she looked up at him. "Yes," she said softly. "I would rather keep on doing it." She turned. "But now you're going to do it, instead, and you still have much to learn." She started up the stairs.

He followed her. "You may find you like it in town," he said.

"You sound like my mother," she replied.

He said nothing. The only sound was the soft tapping of their footsteps as they climbed the steps to the top.

"You'll light the beacon at dusk," Faith said as they came into the tiny tower room. "And keep it lit until dawn." She picked up a cloth from the pile on the ledge. "At least twice a day you should . . ."

But the keeper was paying no attention. He stood at the window, staring out. The sun was low in the west now. It sent a bright path across the water, and each wave reflected the light like a flaming torch.

Faith moved a step to stand beside him.

"I've been on the lake before," he said, almost whispering, "but I've never seen it like this." He couldn't seem to take his eyes from the water.

"Wait till you see it during a storm."

They were both quiet. Faith watched the sparkles of sunlight dancing on the waves far below them. "Look," she said. "See that white triangle?"

"Where?" He turned his head to follow her pointing finger.

"There." She moved so he could see the tiny ship bobbing in the distance. "It's a schooner, heading for the Soo Locks."

"How far out is it?" he said, squinting. "It looks like a toy!"

"Not that far," she said. "Maybe two miles." She faced him, leaning against the railing. "That's the safest distance. Closer in, about there"—she gestured and he looked where she pointed—"are the rocks. The ships need to see our light, so they know when to head toward shore. Too soon and they'll run aground. Too late and they'll miss the entrance to the bay of the Soo."

He nodded, and Faith realized how long it had been since someone had been up here to share this with her. Five whole months. A sudden emptiness threatened to overwhelm her, and tears blurred her view of the lake. She walked to the other side of the tiny room and held her breath. She would not cry. She would *not* cry.

"I can see how much you love this," the keeper said finally, not taking his eyes from the water. "I'm sorry."

Faith shrugged. "It's not your fault," she said, and her voice was almost steady.

She took a deep breath and let it out slowly. "Let me show you how the beacon works," she said, opening the glass door. "This is the heart of the lighthouse."

She went over the working of the light, explaining how he would have to wind the clockworks during the night to rotate the lens so it blinked in the proper sequence. To her relief, he seemed to understand. Now, if only he remembered to order oil.

"Must I wind the clockworks in the middle of the night?" he asked, touching the crank with his finger. "Why doesn't one winding last until morning, like a clock?"

"It's important to keep checking the light," Faith answered, "I've never tried waiting. I never considered the risk worth it."

"Risk?" His brow furrowed.

Faith stamped her foot. "Listen to me," she said, as if she were talking to Willy. "If the light goes out, you put the lives of every sailor on the lake in danger. How can I leave the lighthouse in your care if you don't take that trust seriously?"

"Miss Sutton," he said quietly, "the lighthouse is already in my care, by order of the Lighthouse Board. If you're finished with your tour of the facilities, you're free to go." He smiled at her. "I'll walk with you back to the steamer; the sailors should be just about finished loading your gear."

If he'd struck her it couldn't have hurt more. Faith stepped back. "I know the way out," she said, turning toward the open stairs. Her thoughts churned like the lake in a storm, and her stomach felt like she'd swallowed an anchor. She could hear him behind her, and she ran head-long down the stairs. She burst out of the tower; her quick steps made the planks rattle as she crossed the walkway to the shore. Her mother stood on the landing as two sailors carried the biggest trunk on board the steamer. Her brother danced up the gangway ahead of them.

Faith slowed her pace and adjusted her skirts. She headed toward the landing, and Nathaniel Kent caught up to her. "Miss Sutton?" he said. "Will you wait a moment?"

"Please," Faith interrupted him. "Don't make things worse than they already are. You are lighthouse keeper now." Her voice was steady, and she nodded to the steamer. "As you said, we are about to leave."

"Is there something wrong?" Faith's mother frowned as they approached. "I saw you running across the walkway."

"Nothing's the matter," Faith answered. Nothing you can fix, anyway, she added to herself. "I've told Mr. Kent what he needs to know about the lighthouse."

"They're ready for us to board," her mother said. She touched Faith's arm, motioning her forward.

Faith froze.

Her mother stepped back and gave the new keeper her gloved hand. "It's been a pleasure meeting you," she said. "I hope you have success here." She turned around. "Faith?"

Faith looked at the narrow plank that connected the waiting steamer to the dock. It was only a few steps away. She closed her eyes. I can't do it, she thought.

She sucked in her breath. "May I have a moment?" she asked, turning to her mother.

"Everything's been moved out of the house," her mother said, and Faith could read her impatience in the wrinkle forming between her eyebrows. "All your cases are on board."

"Mother, please." Faith backed away. How could her mother not understand? "Just give me time to say goodbye."

A short toot from the steamer's horn made them all jump. Faith looked up to see Willy grinning from the cockpit. He waved to her. "The ship has a schedule to keep!" he shouted out the window. "Come on!"

Her mother took Faith's hand, gripping it hard as Faith tried to free herself. "You must board now."

"Surely there's a little leeway in the schedule." Nathaniel Kent strode up the gangway. "She's spent all day with me," he called back. "She should have a little time to herself."

"She'll have enough time to herself on board," her mother mumbled, but she waved Faith away. "Go," she said. "But, hurry."

This wasn't the way she'd imagined it, Faith thought. She ran past the house, not daring to go inside. She knew what she'd find: the pile of rags waiting to wipe the lens, her father's boots standing in the corner, the cookstove cold and still. She slowed, and the familiar crunch of sand echoed in her ears as she walked the path to the henhouse.

The hens scurried to her, clucking. "I've nothing for you," she said, and she held out her empty hands. "It's the new keeper you should be watching for."

Their burnished feathers gleamed in the late afternoon sun, and one looked up at her, cocking its head with a bright black eye. It made a funny chirping noise and pecked at an invisible bug on the path.

Faith walked down to the lake. She took off her shoes and stockings and wriggled her feet in the still warm, gritty sand. Out of the corner of her eye she saw her mother wave, but she walked the other way. Let them leave her, she thought.

The beach was scattered with pieces of driftwood washed up in the last storm. She picked up a small twisted stick. Already it was dry, and the gray of the wood was weathered to white. She stroked it; it was almost as smooth as glass.

She watched each wave roll and break on the sand in a soft whoosh of white bubbles. A few steps, and she was standing in the icy water, her skirt wet almost to her knees. The swell of the waves was the slow breathing of the lake, and its rhythm matched the beating of her heart.

She stretched her arms out to the great expanse of emptiness, as if she could be taken into it, taken in and never let go. The way her father had been taken in, she thought suddenly. They had never found his body, just the splintered remains of the lifeboat.

The moving water dragged at her skirts and lapped against her bare legs. She took another step. She knew the bottom dropped off suddenly—a few more feet, and the water would be up to her neck.

But then she looked down the beach toward the lighthouse. She could just barely see her mother, a tiny upright figure standing beside the steamer.

She dropped her arms and waded back to the dry sand. She sat on the rock where her father had taught her how to make knots, pulled her stockings over her wet toes, and slipped her feet into her shoes. She tied the laces and walked up the beach back to the ship.

"Thank you," she said, putting out her hand to the keeper. "Please don't forget to feed the hens."

He raised an eyebrow. "I won't," he said. He bent as if he would kiss her fingers, but she quickly slipped her hand out of his.

"I'm ready," she said to her mother, wishing the lie were truth. She would never be ready.

Her mother nodded. "Let us go, then," she said. And Faith followed her up the gangway to the steamer. As soon as they were on board, the sailors pulled up the plank and the ship moved away from the landing. Faith stood on the deck and watched the lighthouse draw away from her. It grew smaller and smaller, until she thought she would lose sight of it altogether in the dusk.

Then a small light appeared at its tip. It flickered, and suddenly burst out strong and bright, the heartbeat of the lighthouse. It was as if a star had come down to rest on the shore of the lake. She had never seen it from this far away before, but it looked just as she imagined it would. The brightness blurred as her tears fell, but she kept watching until they rounded the bend and headed up the coast for Token Creek. Then it blinked out as suddenly as if it had never been.

Six

"Watch out, you!"

Faith had been watching out for mud puddles; she looked up to see a heavy carriage and two shining black horses bearing down on her.

"Keep your eyes open, girl," the coachman yelled as Faith leaped aside. She landed on her hands and knees in the dirt at the edge of the board sidewalk that ran along the main street of Token Creek. The rattling wheels passed within inches of where she'd just been walking, and the horses' flying hooves tossed clods of mud into her face.

Faith glared at the departing carriage. "Keep *your* eyes open," she echoed back, examining the red scratches on the palms of her hands. She spat a pebble out of her mouth and wished for the thousandth time that she was back at the lighthouse. She closed her eyes. She'd only been in Token Creek for a week, but it seemed like years.

"You deaf or something?" A girl about her own age with wild red hair pulled Faith to her feet and began brushing off her skirt. "Couldn't you hear that carriage coming?"

Faith stepped back. Who *was* this girl, acting if she'd known Faith for years? Faith had never seen her before. She wore a loose brown cotton frock with an apron, not one of those fashionable pencil-thin outfits Faith's cousins loved to show off.

"I guess I did," Faith said, seeing that others on the

street were staring at her. An older woman pulled her bonnet strings tight as she passed by, and a man's face looked out of the window of the store beside her. "I just wasn't expecting to get run over."

The girl grinned. "Well, expect it," she said. "Harlan Chesterfield waits for no man." She shook her head. "And especially for no woman."

"That's Mr. Chesterfield?" Faith spun around, but the carriage was long since out of sight.

"You know him?" The red-haired girl eyed her curiously.

"Not really," Faith answered. Shyness crept upon her, and she groped for something to say. "He represents the Lighthouse Board."

"And you're the lighthouse girl." The red-haired girl put a hand on each of Faith's shoulders, giving her a little shake. "I'm Cassie Kelly," she said, as if that explained everything.

Faith bit her lip. She couldn't even think of what to say to her own cousins when they had come fluttering into the parlor to meet her, much less to this strange girl. "I'm . . . I'm sorry," she stuttered, feeling her face turn red. "Do I know you?"

"Well, of course not," Cassie said. "But I know you. Or," she leaned forward, "I know *of* you. My mam cleans for Mr. Chesterfield. He's always taking about the girl who kept the lighthouse after her father died and how 'in all decency we must get that poor woman and her children out of that inhuman situation.'" Cassie's voice boomed out, obviously imitating Harlan Chesterfield.

Faith laughed, forgetting her shyness for a moment. "That sounds exactly like his letters," she said. "What does he say now that he's finally saved us?"

Cassie pulled on a stray lock of flame red hair. "You

didn't want to be saved, then?" she asked. Her eyes glowed.

"My mother did," Faith murmured, looking down. "I didn't." She examined her mud-soaked shoes. "Right in the puddle," she said, shaking her head. "Mama won't be happy about that."

"I knew it," Cassie crowed. "I told my mam you probably liked it. Living in that little tower with the lake all around . . . not having to go to school. . . ."

"We didn't live in the tower, silly." Faith took Cassie's arm and guided them both up onto the sidewalk. Somehow the red-haired girl's manner let Faith relax. She felt as if she were talking to Willy. "We lived in a house. And we did have school. My mother taught us, and so did my father, before he died. But I did like it." She stopped. If she closed her eyes she could see the tower looming up before her; she could hold her breath and hear the sound of the waves on the beach. She could never explain how she felt about the lighthouse.

"Where are you going?" Cassie skipped along beside Faith. "May I walk with you?"

"My mother needs more nails to hang curtains," said Faith, looking up at the signs above the storefronts lining both sides of the narrow dirt thoroughfare. Their bright colors had mostly faded over the years. "The general store's near here, isn't it?"

"Over there." Cassie grabbed Faith's hand, and they hurried across the street.

"How do you watch out for carriages *and* mud puddles?" Faith asked, hopping over a water-filled rut and up onto the board sidewalk in front of the hotel on the other side of the road. Several men were sitting on a bench outside the entrance; one was talking loudly and gesturing to the sky with a floppy hat, but the others nodded at the two girls as they passed.

Cassie grinned again. "You don't," she said. "You ruin your shoes." She stuck a muddy boot from under her skirt. "Or you wear these."

"I used to go barefoot almost until snowfall," Faith said, thinking of her father's galoshes back at the lighthouse. They would have been just as useful here.

A string of bells jingled when the girls pushed open the door of McDaniel's General Store, one building down from the hotel. As they stepped over the threshold a draft of warm air and the smell of salty pickles and fish enveloped them.

"Be with you in a moment," a voice called out, but its owner was apparently invisible. The floor-to-ceiling shelves were piled with fabric, hardware, bottles, cans, every conceivable necessity. A long U-shaped counter cluttered with boxes and tins ran around three walls of the store, and barrels of crackers and pickles were clustered in one corner. Bridles and harnesses hung from the ceiling. Cassie grabbed a long pole and poked at one of the bridles until it dropped to the floor with a slap.

A round elf of a man popped up behind the counter like a jack-in-the-box. "Cassie Kelly, now you leave that equipment alone," he scolded. "That's the best bridle in the store, and I don't want any nicks on it."

Cassie smoothed the soft leather with her fingers. "How much are you asking, Mr. McDaniel?"

"Too much for you, Cassie girl." Mr. McDaniel laughed. "Besides, you've got a perfectly good bridle for that mare of yours. Now stop your dreaming." Gently he took the bridle from Cassie's hand and put it behind the counter.

Cassie sighed. "This is Faith Sutton, Mr. McDaniel," she said, putting her hand on Faith's shoulder. "She's the lighthouse girl."

Faith stood stiffly as Mr. McDaniel looked her up and

down. She felt like a piece of merchandise he was deciding whether to buy. "Ah," he said, nodding. "We've heard a lot about you, my dear. How do you like living in town?"

Faith forced herself to smile back at him, thinking she would never get used to all these people staring at her and expecting her to speak. Before, on their infrequent visits to town, her mother had always been there to do the talking, but now she was expected to handle this on her own. She searched her mind frantically for something to say. "It's . . . it's very different from the lighthouse," she murmured.

Mr. McDaniel's laugh sounded like the creek that ran behind the keeper's house, bubbling its way to the lake. "Yes, I expect it is," he said. "You're lucky you're here at all. Harlan Chesterfield had a dickens of a time finding a man to replace your father." He wiped his brow with a handkerchief that was only slightly redder than his face. "Now what can I do for you today?"

Faith's mind churned. Lucky! If it was so hard to find a new keeper, why didn't they just let her keep on doing it? But she tried to keep the smile on her face. "My mother needs more nails to hang curtains," she said.

Mr. McDaniel spread a large piece of brown paper on the counter, piled some small nails in the middle, rolled the paper into a neat package, and tied it with string. Faith watched his fingers fly and wondered if he could tie ship's knots as fast. "There you are, miss," he said. "That'll be two cents. Shall I put it on your bill?"

"Please," Faith answered. "My mother said to tell you she'll be getting some money from her father's inheritance. We'll pay you as soon as it comes."

"I'm not worried," Mr. McDaniel answered, nodding as if he knew all about the land and the lumber company's purchase. He made a notation on a slip of paper and put it into the open cash register drawer. "Good day to you," he said. "And stay out of the way of carriages." He winked at Faith, and she wondered if the whole town had seen her near accident.

"Now where?" Cassie asked as they emerged from the store. "More errands?"

Faith held out the package of nails. "Mother's waiting for these. I'd better get home."

"I'll walk with you, then," Cassie said. "I live on Hill Street, one block over from you. It was my mam heard about Mitchells' house for rent and told Mr. Chesterfield. That's your house," she added.

They turned off Main, crossed the town square where an old canon decorated the steps leading to the stone courthouse, and followed a quiet street where big houses were set back from the road and tall trees grew. But when they turned the corner onto Water Street, Cassie grabbed Faith's arm. "Look!" She pointed to the rig standing on the street in front of Faith's front door. "That's Mr. Chesterfield's carriage."

Faith and Cassie looked at each other, eyes wide. "Maybe he's apologizing to Mama for nearly killing me," Faith said, pressing her lips into a determined line.

"Not likely," Cassie retorted. "He's probably suggesting your mother keep you off the road. He has very definite ideas about bringing up girls." She gave Faith's arm a pat. "I'd better be getting on home," she said. "Come visit me. We live just one street over, in the brown house, three from the end." She pointed vaguely ahead of her and walked away down the street.

Faith watched her for a moment, thinking how different Cassie was from Faith's very proper cousins in their fashionably tight skirts. Having a friend like Cassie might not be so bad after all.

Cassie had been right about Mr. Harlan Chesterfield,

Faith discovered a few moments later. He had clearly *not* come to apologize. He stood up and bowed slightly when Faith came into the room, and her mother introduced her. He was not a tall man, but somehow his presence carried an authority that made him seem large in the Suttons' small front parlor. His smile was gentle, his sandy hair was combed perfectly, and he'd placed his hat and gloves just so on the table in the hall. Faith had noticed them particularly when she came into the house. She remembered her father carelessly tossing his keeper's cap on the back of the nearest chair. The thought came with a knife pain in her chest that made breathing difficult.

"Sit down, Faith," her mother began. "Mr. Chesterfield came to suggest that instead of going to public school with Willy, we enroll you in Miss Hutchinson's School for Girls."

Mr. Chesterfield nodded. He sat down and picked up his teacup. "It's new," he said to Faith's mother. "A well-respected institution." His voice was low and musical. "I recommend it highly. The young women of all the best families attend. Music, French, literature . . . Miss Hutchinson develops all the skills necessary for women of society today."

Faith sat with her hands pressed together, holding in the feelings that were threatening to burst out of her. She swallowed, hoping her voice wouldn't crack when she spoke. "Does Cassie Kelly go there?" she asked, knowing the answer.

Mr. Chesterfield's eyebrows shot up. "So you've met Cassie," he said. He turned to Faith's mother. "Cassie's mother does cleaning for me," he said. "She's very efficient. You might want to think about hiring her." He glanced around the room. "When will the closing on your land be? You'll be needing the money before too long, I'd think."

Faith's mother shook her head. "I've hired a lawyer in

Munising to take care of everything," she said, "but I've heard nothing."

"I wonder what's holding it up," he mused, more to himself than anyone else. Then he turned to Faith. "No, my dear," he said, finally answering her question. "I'm afraid Cassie does not attend Miss Hutchinson's school. She has no need of the skills Miss Hutchinson teaches her pupils."

"But you will, Faith," her mother said. She was wearing the white dress that Faith thought made her look like an angel. It wasn't too tight in the front, and the ruffles at the back made Faith think of a waterfall.

Her mother's cheeks were pink, and her eyes sparkled, but Faith recognized that determined line of her mouth. When her mother made up her mind to something, it usually happened. "I think Miss Hutchinson's school sounds like a good idea. You'll have much in common with the other girls there."

Faith watched as her mother stood up to serve tea. She moved so gracefully, she seemed almost to float across the room. They'd rarely had tea at the lighthouse. Faith remembered her father's deep chuckle whenever her mother got out the china teapot and the fragile little cups. It was her mother who would have so much in common with the girls at Miss Hutchinson's, Faith thought.

She blinked back tears. "Do I have to decide right this minute, Mama?" she said, wishing her mother could guess how she felt. She put out her hand to take the cup and saucer her mother offered.

Mr. Chesterfield cleared his throat. "Is it for the child to decide, Elizabeth?" he asked, frowning slightly.

At his words, Faith's hand jerked. The tiny cup seemed to leap off the saucer, but quicker than thought, Faith caught it with her left hand. Hot tea flooded between her fingers and made a brown puddle on the hardwood floor.

Her mother knelt and set the teacup and saucer on the floor. She grabbed Faith's hand. "You're burned."

"It's nothing," Faith mumbled, turning her hand palm up for her mother to see. "The tea wasn't that hot." Mr. Chesterfield's words echoed in her mind. "Elizabeth." How dare he call her mother by her given name.

"Your skin is red," her mother said. "You must put something on it." She turned to Mr. Chesterfield. "What about the doctor, Harlan? Would his surgery be open now?"

Faith felt as if all the breath had been knocked out of her. Mr. Chesterfield was hooking his glasses behind his ears. "Let me have a look," he said.

Faith snatched her hand from her mother's grasp. "I said it's nothing." She jumped to her feet. "I'll put butter on it if that will make you feel better." She stood with her hands behind her, looking from one to the other. They stared at her as if she'd gone out of her mind.

"Faith," her mother said, frowning. "Mind your manners. Whatever is the matter?"

Faith took a breath and let it out, trying to slow the beating of her heart. "Nothing," she said. "I'm just not ready to make a decision about school yet." She glanced at Mr. Chesterfield out of the corner of her eye.

"My dear child," he said. "You have not been reared . . ." He stopped, glanced at her mother, and began again. "Due to the unusual circumstances of your life at the lighthouse," he said, "you have perhaps had more freedom than most girls your age. But you must understand that your parents know what's best for you. It's your parents who will make the decision."

Anger washed over Faith like a bucket of icy Lake Superior water. "Mr. Chesterfield," she said, "I do not have 'parents.'" She spat out the word. "I have one parent.

My mother. And she and I will make our decisions together, as we have done since my father died." There. She'd said it. She felt strong as a fall storm on the lake. "Now good day to you, sir." She stepped toward Mr. Chesterfield, gliding smoothly across the floor. She put out her right hand, and Mr. Chesterfield automatically shook it.

"Good day, Faith," he said, and both his voice and his eyes held a puzzlement that made Faith want to sing. She smiled, lifted her head high, and glided from the room as gracefully as any princess.

She wished she could have sent him from the house, but she knew her mother would never stand for that. Her mother would be angry enough at the way she spoke to the man. Faith knew she was in for a scolding, but for the moment she didn't care. She tossed her hair back over her shoulder with a jerk. It had served him right!

She slowed her footsteps as she rounded the corner, straining to hear what they might say about her. But all was silent. It wasn't until Faith was through the hallway and almost into the kitchen that the murmur of voices began again, and by then she was too far away to hear.

Faith's fingers were throbbing where the hot tea had touched them, and she took butter from the shelf, folded back the cloth it was wrapped in, and began smearing it on her red skin to cool it. Her arms and legs were shaking in reaction, not from the burn—she'd gotten worse from the beacon flames at the lighthouse—but from the thought of her mother and Mr. Chesterfield striking up a friendship.

Faith's heart raced. She closed her eyes and in her mind she saw the white lighthouse tower as she had seen it on the steamer, getting smaller and smaller in the distance. Or was it her mother she saw, moving farther and farther away from her, and from the world Faith loved?

seven

"**Faith?**" **There was a knock** on the door of her room. "May I speak to you a moment?"

Faith jumped at the sound. She looked around, wishing for a place to hide. The last person she wanted to talk to right now was her mother. But she opened the door.

Her mother stood in the hallway with her bonnet on and her cloak over her shoulders.

"We're going somewhere?" Faith asked.

Her mother ignored the question. "May I come in?" she said. Then, not waiting for Faith's reply, she walked past her into the room and sat down on the upholstered stool in front of the vanity. Her mouth was clamped down into the thin line Faith was becoming so familiar with, and her back was ramrod straight.

Faith remembered the story of how her mother had defied her own father and mother, Faith's very proper grandparents, to marry Robert Sutton, and wondered if that was the face she'd used to do it. Well, Faith thought grimly, it wouldn't work with her. She folded her arms and sat down on the bed.

"I want to speak to you about your rudeness to Mr. Chesterfield," her mother said, frowning. "I won't stand for that from my children."

"What about his manners to me?" Faith answered, narrowing her eyes. "He isn't my father. How dare he tell me what to do."

Her mother squeezed her hands together in her lap; her knuckles were white. "You are a child, Faith. There is no excuse for talking to your elders in that fashion."

"I will *not* stand quietly by and let a stranger tell me what I can and can't do," Faith said. "I don't care how old he is."

"Mr. Chesterfield is not a stranger," her mother snapped back. "He's an old friend, and he has taken an interest in you, Faith, because your own father is no longer here to help you."

Faith jumped up. "He's taken an interest in *you!*" Tears stung her eyes, and the lump in her throat made her voice come out in a croak. "He called you Elizabeth!"

Her mother blushed. "I've known Harlan Chesterfield all my life," she answered. "He lived next door to me when we were growing up. Of course he calls me Elizabeth."

The words penetrated slowly. Faith stood in the middle of the room and stared as if her mother were someone she'd never met before. She'd known Mr. Chesterfield all her life? "I don't believe it," she said. "Why haven't you mentioned him before?"

The color rose again on her mother's cheeks. But the expression on her face was stony. "I've had enough of this, Faith. Mr. Chesterfield and I are going to dinner and then to choir practice at the church. I've been asked to play my flute for Sunday service." She stood up. "Until the land is sold, and we can afford a cook, I want you to help prepare the meals. It will be good practice for when you have your own household to run. Tonight you can make potato soup for yourself and Willy. That's his favorite. He's playing next door with his friend, Joseph, and he's to come home by five o'clock."

Faith put her hand on the doorknob, as if she would stop her mother from leaving. "Papa wouldn't stand for it," she said, the words tumbling out in a rush. "It isn't right, you going around with that man. Look at that silly dress. You have to take such little steps; you could never walk on the beach in that."

Her mother's eyes opened wide, and her face went from red to white. "That," she said, lips trembling, "was totally uncalled for. You will stay in your room, young lady, until it's time to fix the soup. Then you will come back here after supper and go straight to bed. And you will think about what it means to be polite and kind."

She grabbed the doorknob and, flinging the door open, walked through, and closed it behind her with a firm final click.

Faith sat down on the bed and stared at the closed door. Her mother had been hurt at the comment about her clothes. "Good," she said aloud, ignoring the tremble in her own voice and the vision of her mother, straight and lovely as a queen in her white dress. "She didn't even ask to see how badly I was burned." She touched her reddened fingers and winced.

"And I *won't* stay in my room!" she whispered. "She can't make me." She stood at the window until she saw the carriage pull away with Mr. Chesterfield and her mother inside. Then she rushed downstairs and grabbed her own bonnet and cloak from the stand in the front hall. There would be plenty of time to talk to Cassie before Willy came home for dinner.

Faith slowed to what she imagined was a sedate pace as she opened the front gate and started up the street. If the neighbors saw her running, they'd surely let her mother know about it. And then she really would be in trouble.

The houses on Water weren't as big as the ones closer to

town, and the front yards were smaller and separated from the street by white picket fences. Most of the yards were full of fall flowers: orange and yellow marigolds and dark red chrysanthemums, and green peony bushes waving their shiny leaves in the wind. She pulled her cloak closer around her. The afternoon was chilly for so soon into September, and the clouds were building up. A storm was blowing in. Out on the lake, she thought, the waves must be gaining strength, probably washing over the walkway. She imagined Nathaniel Kent struggling step by step to the lighthouse, and she hoped he was having trouble. She wished they hadn't left Father's galoshes for him to use.

This was the first storm since Nathaniel Kent had taken over the lighthouse. What if he decides not to cross the walkway? Faith thought suddenly. In her mind she saw the dark lighthouse, and a wind-tossed schooner blown up on the rocks.

Faith took in great gulps of crisp air, trying to get her breath. How would she know what was happening? What if a ship wrecked? What if sailors were drowning? Did she show the new keeper where the lifeboat was? Did he know how to use it? Could he even swim? She couldn't remember if she'd asked him that question. There might have been a million things she'd forgotten to tell him.

She turned down Hill Street, walking so fast that she might as well have been running. If she could just talk to the keeper again . . . but how would she even get to the lighthouse? The steamer wouldn't be going for weeks. She wanted to scream. If it wasn't for Mr. Chesterfield and her mother, she'd be at the lighthouse right now.

Ahead of her was a dilapidated brown house, smaller than the rest on Hill Street. The yard was neatly cared for, with straw mulch over the tiny garden, and the rickety porch was swept clean. This must be Cassie's house, Faith thought. She climbed the steps and knocked at the door. When nobody answered, she knocked again, harder this time. Cassie *had* to be there.

"I'm a-coming," cried a voice from inside. "Hold your horses." The door was flung open by a woman who came only to Faith's shoulder. She had a green bandanna tied around her head, and her face was a mass of wrinkles. But her green eyes twinkled, and the wisp of red hair peeking out from the bandanna labeled her as a relative of Cassie's. "Yes, miss?" The kind eyes were questioning. "What can I do for you?"

Faith swallowed. "Cassie suggested I visit," she said. "Is she here?"

"Bless you," the woman answered, laughing. "She is. Come in." She opened the door wide, and Faith stepped into the front room. There was a heavy ornate sofa on one wall, a huge corner cupboard across from the door, and several chairs lined up against the other walls. The faded rug on the floor had a pattern of vines and flowers. The inside of the house matched the outside—old and obviously worn, but well cared for.

"You must be new in town," the woman said, taking Faith's cloak and bonnet. "I usually recognize all the young ones." She laughed again. "I'm Cassie's mother."

"I'm Faith Sutton," Faith replied. "I'm the lighthouse girl." Somehow this tiny woman put her at ease. Another of Cassie's characteristics, Faith thought.

"Ah." Cassie's mother nodded. "She told me she'd seen you." She opened a door, and Faith could see stairs leading up into darkness. "Cassie," her mother shouted. "Visitor for you."

Immediately Faith heard the staccato of footsteps on the stairs, and Cassie almost tumbled into the room. When she saw Faith, a grin lit up her face. "You came!" She threw her arms around Faith and hugged her as if they'd been apart for months. "Here, let me get my bonnet; we'll go to the stable. I have something to show you." She handed Faith her bonnet and cloak and caught up her own from a pile on one of the chairs.

She grabbed Faith's hand and dragged her out the door. Faith barely had time to nod to the woman who'd greeted her. "Nice to meet you," she called over her shoulder.

"Come again," Cassie's mother said, chuckling.

"I didn't think you'd come so soon," Cassie squealed as they crossed the narrow, tree-lined yard behind the house. At the back was a small stable, its once-red boards weathered to gray. Cassie dropped Faith's hand and slapped her bonnet on her head. The wind was stronger now, and Cassie hastily tied her bonnet strings under her chin. She took a closer look at Faith's face. "What's the matter?"

"I have to tell you something," Faith said. She glanced quickly at the darkening sky and then back to Cassie. "Only, you can't tell anyone we talked about it."

"Of course, I won't," Cassie answered. "I promise."

Faith took a breath. "I've only got a few minutes," she said. "I'm not even supposed to be here." She could feel her face getting hot. "My mother confined me to my room, but I had to talk to you. Something's happened."

Cassie stared at her. "What?" She took Faith's hand and gave it a little shake. "You can tell me. Really."

"Mr. Chesterfield is taking my mother to dinner and then to choir practice at the Methodist Church."

"He *is?*" Cassie's eyes widened, and she sucked in her breath with a little hiss. Her fingers tightened on Faith's, and suddenly Faith found herself telling Cassie the whole story while hot tears gathered in her eyes and rolled down her face.

Cassie loosened her grip on Faith's hand; she stood quietly, an unusually solemn look in her eyes.

"It's true that all the wealthy girls go to Miss Hutchinson's," Cassie said slowly, when Faith stopped for breath. "And the Burleighs are one of the wealthiest families in town." She shook her head. "Your mother is a Burleigh; it's no wonder she wants you to go. You might like it. Your cousin Sarah attends."

Faith scrubbed her wet cheeks with her sleeve. "I won't like it," she said, "especially if Sarah goes there." She glared at Cassie. "She won't even say two words to me; when they came to call she just sat there looking at her long white fingers."

She held out her own hands. Her fingers were squat and square, and still a bit darker in the creases from oil and dirty lighthouse lanterns. "Can you imagine these hands serving tea or playing the piano?" she asked.

Cassie shrugged. "Serving tea's not that hard," she said. "And your mother's right. Someday you'll be a fine lady, and you'll be serving tea whether you like it or not."

"You aren't going to Miss Hutchinson's," Faith fairly shouted at her. "You're not serving tea and learning French."

Cassie giggled. "Now what would I be speaking French for?" she asked. "I'll be a working girl like my mam."

"I won't be speaking French, either," Faith growled. "I'll be tending the beacon at the lighthouse. I'm not going to Miss Hutchinson's school, and that's that."

Cassie grinned. "Good. Then we'll be going to school together. Now come meet Lady." She skipped ahead to the stable, slid the door partway open, and slipped inside.

"Hello, sweet one," she crooned into the darkness.

Faith, who had followed her into the stable, heard an answering neigh, and a stamping of hooves on the dirt floor.

"Do you want a carrot?" Cassie reached into a barrel beside the door and pulled out a limp carrot. She moved to the stall and held out her hand.

As Faith's eyes adjusted to the dim light, she saw a tawny mare put her head over the stall gate and whinny. Her face and neck were the color of honey, and her mane was dark. Delicately she took the carrot from Cassie's open palm and chomped it, bobbing her head as if in appreciation.

"Isn't she beautiful?" Cassie whispered, rubbing the mare's neck and running her fingers through her long forelock. "This is Lady." She gestured to Faith with one hand. "Lady, this is my friend, Faith."

Lady kept bobbing her head, and Faith wasn't sure whether she was acknowledging the greeting or asking for another carrot. "Nice to meet you, Lady," Faith said.

"Give her a carrot," Cassie suggested.

Faith reached her hand into the darkness of the barrel. Her fingers closed around a cold carrot. "Here, Lady," she said, presenting the carrot to the horse.

"Hold your hand flat," Cassie explained. She grabbed Faith's hand and stretched out her fingers so the carrot was resting on her palm. "Now she can eat it without biting you."

Faith felt the whisper of the mare's breath tickling her palm. The soft lips nipped up the carrot. Then Lady whinnied, bobbing her head again.

"She likes you," Cassie said. "Do you ride?"

"I never have," Faith said. "But I bet I could do it."

"Of course you could." Cassie grabbed the bridle hanging just outside the stall. "I'll teach you."

"Not today," Faith said. She gritted her teeth. "I have to get back to make dinner for Willy."

Cassie turned. "Because your mother and Mr. Chesterfield . . . ?"

Faith nodded. Her throat tightened with unshed tears, but she held her breath, trying not to cry. What would Cassie think of her?

But at that moment, Faith heard a small voice call out, "Faith?"

She rushed to the stable door. "I'm here, Willy," she said, stepping outside. "Are you all right?"

Willy's eyes were round in his thin face. "Where's Mama?" he said, his voice quivering.

"She'll be back," Faith said, giving her brother a hug. "How did you find me?"

"Joseph's mother saw you walking," he explained. "Why did you go away?"

"Come see what's in here," Faith said, unwilling to answer his question. She took his hand and drew him into the stable.

She watched his eyes widen even more when he caught sight of Lady. "What a beauty," he whispered, taking a step toward her.

"Move slowly," cautioned Cassie, touching his shoulder. "Don't startle her."

"I won't," he said, keeping his voice low. "Can I pet her?"

"You may give her a carrot." Cassie plopped one on his open palm and showed him how to feed the horse. "Are you Willy?"

He nodded, keeping his eyes on Lady. "And I know you're Cassie."

"How did you know that?" Faith asked him, surprised.

"All the kids know Cassie," Willy explained. Lady lowered her head and sniffed Willy's blond hair with wide, quivering nostrils, and he giggled.

Out the stable door Faith could see the branches of the trees moving in the wind. "Storm's coming," she said.

Cassie stepped out the door. "Willy's here now. How about a riding lesson?"

Faith saw Willy's face light up. She followed Cassie outside and sniffed the wind. "There's not enough time," she said. "It'll be raining in half an hour. Lots of wind, too." She closed her eyes, feeling the breeze on her cheek. If she could just *see* the lighthouse tower, to know if he'd lit the lamp, then it would be easier to be so far away.

Cassie peered up at the sky. "Thirty minutes? How do you know that? Half the sky's still clear."

"Lighthouse keepers know lots of things," Willy explained. He took Faith's hand.

Cassie was still looking at the clouds. "I think you must be right," she said. "They're coming fast." She smiled at Faith. "How handy to know about storms. You'd never get caught out in one."

Faith and Willy looked at each other and laughed. "Lighthouse keepers are *supposed* to go out in storms," Faith said. "To light the lamps."

"Oh." Cassie thought for a moment. "Is it fun?"

Faith nodded. "But I don't think it would be the best time to learn to ride a horse."

"You're probably right," Cassie answered. "Storms don't bother Lady much, though." She shut the stable door. "I'll walk home with you."

The wind was rising, and the image of the darkened lighthouse was clearer in Faith's mind than Cassie and Willy, who were standing right beside her. Were the waves over the walkway yet? She touched Cassie's shoulder. "Is there any place in Token Creek where we could see the lighthouse?"

Cassie stared at her friend. "I don't think so," she said. "Why?"

Faith shrugged. "I just want to see it, that's all." It did

sound silly, she thought. To worry about a lighthouse.

They walked down Hill Street, turned the corner onto Park, and walked a block to Water. Suddenly Cassie stopped. "If you let me teach you to ride Lady," she pointed out, "maybe we could ride there someday. There's supposed to be a path along the bluff." She held out her hand and caught a big wet splat of raindrop on her fingers. "Here comes the rain," she said. "But I'm still going to get wet, even if I cut through Simpsons' yard." She tied her bonnet strings tighter and headed across the back garden toward Hill Street.

Faith watched the pine branches bending the wind and listened to Cassie's words echoing in her ears. Maybe she *could* get to the lighthouse after all.

"Come on, Willy," she said, taking him by the shoulders and giving him a push toward the house. "Let's find some of those fat potatoes for the soup."

eight

It was during their third riding lesson that Cassie showed Faith the path to the lighthouse. "Maybe we could take a picnic there sometime," she said.

Faith took a firm grip on Lady's reins and stared at the faint trail. It wound along the rocky bluff that marked this part of Lake Superior's southern shore. She had never been allowed to walk on top of the bluffs when they lived at the lighthouse. They were altogether too crumbling and dangerous, her mother had always said. But maybe her mother was wrong. She peered into the darkness beneath the trees. The forest that separated the Port Henry Lighthouse from the town of Token Creek was thick, and grew almost to the edge of the bluff. "How far do you think it is?" she asked.

"Mr. McDaniel said three or four miles," Cassie answered. "He used to fish along the shoreline when he was a boy. He said you can't get through walking on the beach, but the bluff trail might be passable." They'd been riding double with Cassie behind, and she slid off Lady's broad back. "Tie Lady to that tree, and let's walk along it."

Faith dismounted, swinging her leg up and over Lady's back. She loved wearing the old pair of men's trousers Cassie had found for her. But her mother would be scandalized if she knew.

"Goodness, it's steep here," said Cassie. They stood together, looking down to the water about a hundred feet below. The sandy cliffs were streaked with reddish brown, as if some giant had spilled a huge can of paint. Here and there small caves made pockmarks in the smooth surface. Cassie picked up a stone and heaved it out into the great expanse of lake and sky. It seemed like a long time before Faith heard the faint plop and saw the tiny ring of ripples where it landed.

"This is a little like being in the lighthouse," Faith said. She gestured behind her. "But picture the lake all around you."

Cassie squinted, as if she were trying to imagine it. "No wonder you didn't want to leave," she said.

Faith moved ahead along the path, which wound alternately beneath the trees and right out to the cliff edge. "Watch your step here," she cautioned, grabbing a branch of a big pine tree for support. "If you slipped on these rocks . . ." She left the sentence unfinished, and her gaze followed the tumbling of a pebble as it bounced to the water.

"Lady could pick her way," Cassie assured her. "We'd just give her her head."

"Maybe we could try it now," Faith said, looking at the sun. Was there time enough? The path turned away from the bluff into the trees, and she walked on a few steps. Maybe if they went a little farther she could at last see the lighthouse.

"Wait, Faith," Cassie said, following her. "It'll be dark soon. And we'd be crazy to do it in the dark. Even on Lady."

Faith turned. "How about Saturday, then?"

Cassie shook her head. "I have to help my mam on Saturday." She leaned against a tree, considering the problem. "If only we didn't have school."

"At least we're in the same school," Faith pointed out.

She had simply refused to go to Miss Hutchinson's. "It would be a disaster," she'd said, ignoring her mother's angry look. "I know it would."

"Well," her mother had said at last. "You can't attend, anyway, until the land is sold. We couldn't afford to pay the tuition." Her eyes had strayed to her flute case on the table by the piano. "Your life is so different from what I knew when I was growing up," she'd said, and her voice had trembled slightly.

Faith's anger had melted. She'd knelt by her mother's chair and put her arms around her mother's waist. "I'm so sorry I'm not like you," she'd whispered.

Her mother had put her cheek against Faith's hair in a gesture that had made Faith want to cry. "I wish your father were here," her mother had said, so low that Faith could hardly hear her. "He'd know what to do."

Faith had wished it, too. But she had also silently thanked the Lord for whatever was holding up the land deal in Munising.

She was enrolled in Horace Mann Public School. It wasn't quite as bad as she'd expected. The teacher placed her at the back of the room, where she couldn't feel the others looking at her. Cassie was in her class. And they could go horseback riding after school on days when the weather was fine.

Now Cassie threw another pebble. "It would be better to picnic in the summertime," she said, watching as the pebble arched over the edge of the cliff and down into the water. "It gets dark so early now."

"Maybe we'll get a day off," Faith answered. She looked out, straining to see the lighthouse. But it was lost in the distant blue of the sky and the water. "By summer it will be too late. Who knows what will happen before then."

Cassie shook her head. "Stop worrying," she said. "Nat thinks too much of his own good looks, but he's smart. He'll do all right."

"Nat?" Faith frowned.

"Nat Kent," Cassie said. "The new lighthouse keeper."

"You know him?"

"Of course I know him." Cassie grinned. "Everybody knows everybody in Token Creek. He's Mr. Chesterfield's nephew. He left school in the East and needed a job." She shrugged. "Something about not keeping his grades up."

Faith's eyes went wide. "So they let him be keeper?" She jumped to her feet. "Mr. Chesterfield's nephew?"

Cassie stood up. "It'll be all right, Faith. He's not a bad sort."

"But lighthouse keeper?" She could hardly keep from screaming. "My father died trying to save a ship from sinking." She gestured to the lake. "Would Nathaniel Kent do that?"

Cassie considered, seemingly unperturbed by Faith's shouts. "I don't know him that well," she said. "Maybe not."

"That's what I'm worried about." Faith gritted her teeth and started walking on down the path. "Has he fixed the walkway? Does he even know how to swim?"

"Faith, wait!" Cassie called after her. "You can't go now. It's getting dark. And besides," she caught up to Faith, "why don't you let Mr. Chesterfield worry about it now?"

Faith spun around. "I wish he'd just disappear," she said. "If it weren't for Mr. Chesterfield, I'd *be* at the lighthouse right now. And I wouldn't have all these problems."

Cassie touched her arm. "But they're not your problems now," she said. "Can't you just stop thinking about it?"

Faith's shoulders slumped, and she rubbed her forehead. She closed her eyes and swallowed back her tears. "My father said over and over that keeping the beacon lit is more important than anything else. And when I remember all those sailors out on the lake, searching for the light . . ." She looked at Cassie. "Have you ever seen a schooner with its masts all twisted and broken, washing up onto the rocks? Have you seen seven dead bodies lined up side by side on the shore, waiting for people to bury them?"

Cassie shook her head.

"I have," she said. "I was the one who pulled some of them out of the water." She stopped, remembering how she'd dragged one man up onto the sand. She'd grabbed his shoulders, shaking him and shaking him, screaming at him to open his eyes. "He was so heavy," she whispered. "Even his arms were heavy."

She turned, suddenly realizing Cassie was standing beside her, staring. "And none of them was my father's body. We didn't even get to bury him," she said. "We just never saw him again."

Cassie put her arm around Faith's waist.

"I can't sleep at night in town," Faith continued. "I keep waking up. At first I think the beacon's gone out, and I start to jump up." She shook her head. "And then I remember we're not at the lighthouse anymore."

Cassie took Faith's hand, and slowly they began to walk back to the tree where they'd tied Lady. "But it won't help to go back now, will it?"

Faith wiped her eyes with the sleeve of the old wool jacket she was wearing. "If I could just see the lighthouse," she said. "If I could just talk to the keeper, to make sure everything's all right. Then maybe . . ." She shrugged. "When I was keeper, at least I was doing something. I was keeping the light lit. Now . . ." She spread her hands in the empty air and left the sentence unfinished.

Cassie mounted Lady, and Faith pulled herself up behind her. "I have an idea," Cassie said. "Maybe you can get to the lighthouse after all."

Faith's heart gave an extra hard beat that was almost painful. "How?" she asked. She wrapped her arms around Cassie's waist. Cassie tapped Lady's sides with her heels, and they started off at a trot.

"You can take Lady and go there tomorrow." Cassie glanced back at Faith.

"But what about school?"

"I'll say you're sick. I'll bring your work home to you." She clucked to the horse, and Lady broke into a slow canter. "It's Friday, and we never do much on Friday. You can ride out, talk to Nat, and then ride back. Just be home about the time school's out. How would anyone ever know?"

Would that work? Could she play hooky from school and go to the lighthouse? "What about Willy?" Faith asked. "He'd know."

Lady's hooves sounded like thunder as they crossed the wooden bridge over Token Creek and came into town the back way. Cassie was silent for a moment. "Maybe you can let him in on it," she suggested. "He wouldn't tell on you, would he?"

Faith shook her head. "I don't think so," she said, "unless someone asked him outright. He couldn't lie."

"Who'd ask him?" Cassie waved her hand in the air. "I wouldn't say you were very sick. You just have a headache and need to rest for a day." She turned and gave Faith a sad look. "You poor thing. Such a bad headache."

Faith laughed. "It just might work," she said. "Do I ride well enough?"

Cassie nodded. "If I didn't think so," she said, "I'd never let you take Lady. But you mostly know what you're doing, and Lady always knows what she's doing. It's a good match."

That settled it. Faith changed her clothes in the stable, leaving the pants and jacket there for the morning. Cassie promised to leave a bag of carrots for Lady. "What will the weather be like?"

Faith sniffed the air. "It doesn't smell like a storm," she said. "I think it might be cold in the morning. But it'll warm up by lunchtime."

"Perfect," Cassie said.

"I hope so," Faith answered. If it wasn't, she'd be in more trouble than she cared to think about.

nine

There was a skim of ice on the watering trough outside the stable the next morning when Faith and Lady began their trek to the lighthouse. Lady's breath whooshed out in a steamy cloud, and the grass at the sides of the road looked like furry fingers of frost. But the sky was blue as a sapphire, with not even a wisp of cloud. It would be a fine day.

They had cornered Willy as he came out the door and promised him a ride on Lady, all by himself, if he'd be quiet. "I won't touch the reins," Cassie had said. "I'll even show you how to gallop."

Faith thought that was going a little too far, but decided not to think about it now. Trotting would probably be plenty fast enough for Willy.

"But what if somebody asks me," he'd said at the last, eyes wide and worried. "It's a sin to lie."

Faith had looked at his thin, scared face and wished he was the happy-go-lucky child he'd been before he'd gotten sick. Before Papa died. "Nobody will ask you," she'd assured him. "Why would they? Does anybody ask about me now?"

Willy had shaken his head. "Did they before I went to school?"

"No."

Faith could still hear skepticism in his voice. "You can tell if somebody asks," she'd said. "Somebody important."

He'd nodded, obviously relieved. "See if my fort's still safe," he'd said to Faith, "and tell the keeper he can sit there, but don't wreck it."

Now, as she crossed the bridge over Token Creek, Faith had a vivid image of Nathaniel Kent crouched in the fort Willy and their father had built out of old pine branches and a couple of ancient ship's timbers that had washed up on the beach. "Not likely," she said, and one of Lady's ears twitched back at the sound.

Lady had no problem following the path along the bluff. It was harder for Faith. When the trail passed among the trees, she had to duck, sometimes riding flat against the mare's back to keep from being brushed off by low branches. But that wasn't as scary as when the path came close to the cliff edge. Lady picked her way, step by step, through the rocks. Faith closed her eyes, or looked out at the sparkling waters of Lake Superior. She tried not to listen to the sound of the stones tumbling down to the water as Lady's hooves loosened them.

"This isn't so bad," Faith said to Lady.

Lady's ear cocked back as if to listen.

Faith held the reins loosely and gave the mare's smooth neck a pat. "We're not in a hurry," she said. "Just take your time." She squinted, checking the position of the sun. It was still low; it was not more than half past eight o'clock. She had the entire day still ahead of her, and she was going to be at the lighthouse.

"Alone!" she said, triumphant. Both Lady's ears went back at that.

"Well," she added, "not exactly alone." The new keeper would be there. "He'd better be there," she muttered. "If he's not, I'll get him fired."

Lady's ears flicked forward, and they rode on. The only noise besides the birds calling to one another was the sound of the mare's hooves thumping in the dirt under the trees and crunching the stones nearer the cliff.

The sun climbed a little higher in the sky, and Faith slipped off the heavy wool jacket she'd put on over the rough shirt Cassie had taken from her mother's ragbag. Suddenly Lady turned, even though the path appeared to be going straight.

"What are you doing, Lady?" Faith asked her. She pulled on the reins, and the horse immediately stopped. "Why are you going that way?" She pointed. "The path goes straight." She touched the mare with her heels, but instead of taking a step forward, Lady again headed left, into the woods.

"Whoa," Faith called. She looked carefully at the path, which led across a sandy place close to the edge of the bluff. Why wouldn't Lady follow it?

She tapped Lady's sides again, and the horse started off toward the woods. "Well," Faith said. "Cassie said to let you choose the way." She shrugged and let the horse go where she would.

Lady followed an alternate path that apparently only she could see. They went through the trees and then back out to the bluff on the other side of the sandy soil. Faith looked back, trying to figure out Lady's problem with that section of the path. It seemed safe enough, but Cassie had said Lady always knew what she was doing. And Faith believed Cassie. She sighed and turned around.

There in front of her was the white finger of the lighthouse, pointing toward the sky. Faith caught her breath, and it was all she could do not to kick Lady, frantically hurrying her on. The black roof gleamed, reflecting the morning sun like the beacon itself. The harsh cries of the seagulls sounded like music; she realized she hadn't heard that familiar screeching since she'd left the lighthouse. Were there no seagulls at Token Creek, or had she just not been listening?

The next half hour was both agony and ecstasy. Faith could see the lighthouse getting closer and closer, but the path angled down the bluff in a series of switchbacks; she was afraid to move or even breathe lest Lady lose her footing.

When they were finally walking on the beach, Faith heaved a sigh of relief, and she laughed when Lady sighed, too. Faith touched her heels to Lady's flanks, and the mare broke into a trot, skimming over the stretch of hard sand between the bluff and the lighthouse.

They passed Willy's fort, and when they reached the walkway, Faith stopped. The place seemed deserted. Where was the keeper? She dismounted and led Lady up the beach to the boathouse and tied her to the post that held the lantern.

She took one quick look toward the house and headed for the tower, but before she'd gotten to the walkway, she heard a door bang shut.

"Hey! What's going on?"

Faith turned to see the new keeper coming toward her, pulling the coat of his uniform on as he hurried along. She stood and waited for him, suddenly aware that she had no idea what she was going to say.

"Who are . . . ," the keeper began, and Faith saw his eyes widen as he recognized her. "Oh," he said. "It's you." He twitched his shoulders to settle the coat. It was her father's old one and, as she'd predicted, it was too big for him. He frowned, and then, remembering his manners, held out his hand. "Miss Sutton," he said, "I wasn't expecting a visit."

Faith touched his fingers with her own and then drew back. "I hope you don't mind," she said, her thoughts racing. "It was . . . a rather abrupt decision."

"Not at all," he answered, looking perplexed. "But how . . ." He saw the horse, and turned back to her. "You rode here?" He sounded incredulous.

Faith nodded. "A friend let me borrow her horse."

The keeper looked again at the horse and then back at Faith. "That's Cassie Kelly's mare," he said, eyebrows raised. "You must be a pretty fair rider if Cassie trusts Lady to you." He looked impressed.

Faith had forgotten that Nathaniel Kent knew Cassie. She nodded, but found she couldn't let the lie stand. "I think she trusts the horse," she said, shrugging.

The keeper smiled. "That, too," he said. There was a long pause. He cleared his throat. "May I ask the reason for your visit?"

"I just . . ." She stopped, trying to collect her thoughts. "I just wondered how you were doing," she said. She wanted to kick herself when she heard how plaintive the words sounded. "I thought maybe you had more questions, now that you've been here awhile." She glanced to the lighthouse and back again. "You are lighting the lamp, aren't you?"

She saw a flash of irritation cross his face. "Yes," he answered, with exaggerated patience. "I've been lighting the lamp. Every night," he added, leaning slightly forward. "Would you like to go up?"

"I would," Faith said. She took a deep breath, trying to stop the sudden pounding of her heart. Nathaniel Kent motioned for her to precede him, and they headed for the lighthouse.

"Did the walkway get fixed?" she asked him.

"Not yet," he said. "Your temporary railing is working fine."

"But it won't hold." She stopped, and he came up

beside her. "You've got to fix it before the storms start."

"I had no trouble at all during the last one," he said. "You don't have enough confidence in your own handiwork." He grinned, as if she should be pleased at the compliment.

"You don't understand," she said, trying to keep calm. "The storms will get much worse before too long. It will soon be dangerous for you to cross the walkway unless it's fixed permanently."

"It's good of you to be so concerned with my safety." Nathaniel Kent nodded.

Faith studied the tall lighthouse tower. "I'm concerned that you can get to the lighthouse to light the lamps," she answered.

The keeper shrugged. They walked single file along the walkway. Faith stopped to check the knots. They were holding, it was true. But he had no idea of the fury of the lake in November.

"I did mention it to my uncle," Nathaniel Kent said. "He indicated there was plenty of time."

They reached the door to the lighthouse. Faith put her hand on the heavy doorknob, and then looked back at the keeper.

He had a strange look on his face, an embarrassed half smile. "I'll let you open the door, if you don't mind."

Faith laughed in spite of herself. She opened the door and walked into the lighthouse, and the keeper followed her. "Mr. Kent," she said as they climbed the steps, "your uncle has a habit of leaving things to the last minute, as far as the lighthouse is concerned. He was *always* saying there was plenty of time. Even when we knew there wasn't."

She looked back at him; his face was impassive. "I wish you'd let me be the judge of that," he said. "I *am* the keeper now."

She ground her teeth together. How could she make him understand? But as she rounded the last bend and stepped into the tower room, her frustration melted away like ice on a summer day. The lake lay before her, an unbroken expanse of blue that turned invisibly into the sky, transforming the whole world into an enormous blue vault with Faith at the very center. In the whisper of waves on the shore she heard the beating of her heart, and she felt the rhythm giving her life. Or was it Faith, giving life to the rhythm of the waves? She couldn't tell which was powering which.

The keeper's slight cough sounded loud as a gunshot, and she jumped. "What do you think?" he asked.

She turned, and saw that he was looking at the lens itself. It hadn't a smudge or stain on it. "It looks clean," she said, nodding. Actually, it looked more than clean. Both the beacon and the room were spotless. "You're doing a good job with it."

The keeper laughed. "Do I detect some grudging respect?" he said. "Or at least approval?" He leaned back against the brass railing that ran around the edge of the tiny room.

Faith stared at him for a moment, and then, not being able to help it, she grinned. After all, she was standing in her favorite place in the whole world. How could she not smile? "Approval," she answered. "A tiny bit of approval."

The keeper shook his head. "You're a hard taskmaster, Miss Sutton." He turned, heading down the steps. "When you're ready, I do have some questions." He disappeared, leaving Faith alone in the blue vault.

She gazed out the windows until the sun reflecting off the water nearly blinded her. And then she went down the steps. It would have been perfect, except she wished it were her father waiting below instead of Nathaniel Kent.

He'd put the cloth bag she'd tied to Lady's saddle, as well as a pitcher of water and two glasses, on the flat boulder she'd always used as a bench. He also had a length of rope. "Ready for lunch?" he asked. "It's almost noon." He motioned for her to sit down. "I hope you don't mind me setting things up."

Faith swallowed hard, remembering all the times she had eaten lunch with her father sitting just like this on the very same boulder. What gave Nathaniel Kent the right . . . ?

She bit her tongue on the sharp words she was about to say. After all, it wasn't his fault.

"Noon already?" she said, instead. She glanced at the sun, which was straight overhead. "I've got to be getting back soon."

"Why?" The keeper poured water in the two glasses and handed her the bag in which she'd packed her lunch. He had a cold potato and a loaf of bread on a metal plate. He must have brought the plate with him; Faith knew it had not belonged to the lighthouse.

"School's over at three, and it takes almost two hours to ride back," Faith said. She sat down and drank an entire glass of water without stopping. Even the water tasted different in town.

"They excused you from school?" The keeper poured her another glass of water.

Faith suddenly realized what she'd almost admitted to. "Not exactly," she said, blushing.

The keeper's eyebrows went up. He took a bite of his potato, chewed it carefully, and swallowed. "You mean nobody sent you here?"

Faith shook her head, surprised. "Why would anyone send me?"

The keeper's smile was rueful. "I thought maybe my uncle was checking up on me," he said. Then he chuckled.

"Though I should have guessed anyone he sent wouldn't have come attired so . . . informally."

Faith suppressed the urge to glance down at the men's trousers she was wearing, but she felt her face go red. "It's easier to ride this way." She kept her eyes trained on the far horizon of the lake. "Why would your uncle check up on you?" she asked him, and then remembered he'd flunked out of college.

He shrugged. "My uncle isn't the most trusting soul," he said.

Some gulls gathered at the water's edge, eyeing the remains of the meal. Faith threw them the last pieces of her bread, and they squabbled over it, screeching and pecking at each other for the tiny crumbs. "They're so greedy," Faith said. "I always had to chase them off so the hens could eat their grain."

The keeper cleared his throat. "Do you think you could show me that knot you used on the railing before you go?" He picked up the rope. "Just in case the walkway doesn't get fixed in time."

Faith looked at the sun; it had moved a little bit from the zenith. And she looked at the keeper, waiting, twisting the rope between his fingers. "I think I could," she said. "It's not hard." At least he was trying to be responsible. He couldn't help it that his uncle hadn't sent the materials for the walkway. "If I had some wood it would be easier to see how it works."

He put his arms out, one on top of each other as if they were two overlapping sticks. "Pretend this is the wood," he said. "Just promise to untie me when you're done." He winked at her.

She laughed. "If you promise to get the walkway fixed, I'll untie you." She wrapped the rope around his arms, threading it carefully. "Over here," she said, pointing, "and then under here. And then pull it tight." She looked at him. "See?"

He examined the knot, testing the strength of it. "Take it off and do it again," he said. "I'm not sure I understand."

She retied the knot, slower this time, and he nodded. Then she did it once more. "Now you try it," she said, holding out her own arms.

For once he didn't make a joke, and his expression was absorbed. "Under here and over . . ." He shook his head and untied the knot. "No, that's wrong." He wrapped the rope around her wrists once more. "Over here and *then* under." He pulled the knot tight. "I did it!" He looked as pleased as Willy had.

Faith smiled. "Good." She tried to wiggle free of the knot and couldn't. "It's tight." She held her arms out so he could untie her.

"You're lucky I'm such a gentleman," he said, keeping his hands in his lap. "I could just leave you tied there."

Faith stared at him. "You'd better not," she said. Her stomach suddenly felt like she'd eaten a lump of lead. Would he try that?

"Why not?" he asked her. "It's lonely here. I'd like some company."

"But not company who lectures you day and night." She held out her arms again. "If you want some peace, you'd better untie me."

"You're right," he said, and undid the knot. "Can you wait while I try it on the walkway?"

She stood up and brushed the rest of the crumbs from her lap. "I'm not sure how long it took me to get here," she said. "I've got to get back before . . ."

"Before they find out you're gone?" He put his arm under her elbow and urged her toward the lighthouse. "This won't take long." He trotted out onto the walkway, planks clattering at each step. She followed him. Quickly he tied one knot, and then another. "Is that right?"

"Exactly," she said. "I couldn't have done it better myself." She looked up at the tower. "Now I've got to go."

"I'll get Lady," he said. "You can go up once more if you want."

She flashed him a grateful look and ran to the lighthouse. She climbed the steps two at a time and, at the top, took a last long look around. "I wish I could paint," she said, wondering if anyone could capture the view from the tower the way she saw it.

The keeper was giving Lady another long drink from the lake. "Thanks for coming," he said, when Faith was once more standing on the sand. He looked down at her. "I was serious when I said it's lonely around here."

Faith took the reins, thinking it would most likely be a long time before she could come again. She looked back at the lighthouse tower and then out to the lake. It was lonely, yes, but she'd give anything to be here. "You might get used to it," she said.

"I can help you mount." He leaned down. "Put your foot in my hand." When she did, he boosted her into the saddle. "I'm glad my uncle didn't send you."

"Me, too." She grinned at him. "I just hope I get back before school lets out. Come on, Lady; let's go." She touched her heels to Lady's flanks, and they took off, heading for the path at a trot.

ten

Faith took the back road into town, past some broken-down sheds, behind the livery stable and the big haystack beside it. The road turned, and she guided Lady through a stand of pines that backed up to the stable. She couldn't tell whether school had let out, because from here it was impossible to know if the boys were playing ball in the street. But the sun was still high enough; it appeared she was in time.

She dismounted, but before she could take two steps to push on the stable door, it flew open. Cassie stood there, eyes wide, hair even more disheveled than usual. Faith stared at her. Her heart felt like it had suddenly dropped into her shoes.

"Finally!" Cassie rushed out and grabbed Lady's bridle.

"What's happened?" Faith gripped her friend's arm. "What time is it?"

Cassie pulled Lady inside, and Faith followed. She stepped into the stable and was nearly knocked over as Willy threw his arms around her and hugged with all his might.

"Please don't be angry. I didn't know what to say. I couldn't help it." His voice, muffled by her baggy wool pants, trembled, and he started to cry. "And now I won't get to ride Lady all by myself."

Faith patted Willy's shoulders, but her hands were shaking. She looked over at Cassie, who was unsaddling Lady.

"There was a chimney fire at the school," Cassie said. Her voice was flat. "We always get one or two in the fall, when we first light the stove." She shook her head. "But of all the rotten luck, to have one today."

"The school burned down?" Faith was shocked.

Willy looked up at her. "No, silly," he said. "It was such a mess with cinders all over, so they dismissed us early. Before lunch."

Faith's legs suddenly couldn't hold her up. She plopped down on the dirt floor. "And when you got home, Mama asked you where I was," she said.

Willy nodded. "You said if somebody important asked, I should tell." His eyes were big. "And there's nobody more important than Mama."

"Oh, Willy . . ." Faith put her head in her hands. "Why didn't you tell her I was at Cassie's?"

Cassie had started brushing Lady. "That's what I asked him," she said. "He came running over here after lunch. He was so pale, I thought he would faint."

Willy crawled into Faith's lap and looked up at her. "I didn't think of it," he said, his eyes sad.

Faith stroked his hair. "Were you scared?" she asked. "What did Mama say?"

"Her mouth went into a line," he said, pressing his lips together to demonstrate. "You know, that way she does when she's mad? She made me tell her everything, about the horse and everything."

"And then what happened?"

"She went up to her room," Willy answered. "And I came here."

"You've been here all afternoon?"

Cassie had gone out to pump some water for Lady and came back with a full bucket. "We tried and tried to think what to do," she said. "But it was hopeless." She shrugged.

Faith nodded, wondering whether her mother was home. She closed her eyes.

Willy touched her shoulder. "What are you going to do?"

Faith made a wry face. "Go live at the lighthouse?"

Cassie laughed, and Willy's eyes went wide. "Could you?"

Faith shook her head. "I wish I could," she said. The words seemed to hang in the air, bouncing from wall to wall in the stable before fading away. "Was anybody hurt in the fire?"

Willy shook his head. "The fire department came." He jumped up. "But the fire was out by then. Ben Nichols climbed up on the roof and dumped salt down the chimney."

"That sounds like something Ben would do," Faith said. Ben was the oldest boy in school, and the craziest. He'd flunked at least one grade. Rumor had it that he was sweet on the teacher, and it might be true; she wasn't much older than he.

Faith stood up. "Willy, run home now, and see if Mama's there." He headed for the door, but Faith stopped him. "If it's okay with Cassie, you'll still get to ride."

Willy grinned and shut the door behind him when he left.

Faith slipped off the riding pants and the shirt and put her dress back on. Cassie buttoned her up in the back. "The boys get whipped when they skip school," she said, almost whispering.

"What would happen to a girl?" Faith clenched her hands into fists. Let them try to whip her.

Cassie shook her head. Her eyes were as wide as Willy's. "I don't know. The girls never skip."

Faith laughed. "Leave it to me to do something no girl has ever done before." She tried to smooth back her hair. "Maybe they'll banish me to the lighthouse." She gave Cassie a hug. "Whatever happens, at least I got to see it one more time. Thank you for letting me ride Lady."

"Was Nat there?"

Faith nodded. "He's keeping it all clean. He must be lighting the light. He knew your horse, and he thought I must be a good rider for you to trust me with Lady." Faith laughed. "I didn't tell him I've only had three lessons."

Cassie smiled. "You are a good rider," she said. "Do you like Nat better now?"

Faith raised an eyebrow. "Not much. He hasn't fixed the walkway yet." She turned to go. "I might as well get this over with." She folded her arms across her chest to make herself feel strong, and started home.

As she rounded the corner of Water Street, she heard the high notes of her mother's flute trilling out an open window. Then a man's voice sang, low and smooth, and the flute sound soared above it. Faith stopped at her front door to listen; the music gave her shivers. The two voices, the man's and the flute's, wove patterns, an invisible lacy design of swirls and circles that filled the air around her and took her breath away.

And then it was over. There was the low rumble of Mr. Chesterfield's speaking voice, and her mother's soft laugh. Faith sighed. It would be hard enough to talk to her mother alone, but with Mr. Chesterfield there, who knows what would happen. With hands that were not quite steady, she pushed open the door and went into the house.

The sudden silence was so thick, it felt solid. Faith wondered where Willy was. Slowly she took off her cloak and bonnet and hung them on the hooks by the long hall mirror. She smoothed her hair, took a deep breath, let it out in a whoosh, and went into the front parlor.

Her mother had put aside her flute and was sitting with her hands folded in her lap. She was wearing the white dress that made her look so fragile, almost not a part of the world at all. And certainly not a part of the lake world Faith loved.

Mr. Chesterfield, with his hands in his pockets, was leaning up against one of the tall columns that framed the fireplace.

"Sit down, Faith." Her mother nodded to an empty chair across from the one she occupied. The firm line of her mouth told Faith things would go badly if she refused. She pressed her own lips together and sat down.

"Willy tells me you were not in school today."

"No, Mama." Faith looked at the floor. "I went to the lighthouse."

Her mother stood. "Faith, how could you?" She raised her arms and then dropped them to her sides. "Skipping school? Riding out unchaperoned to spend the day with a man?"

Faith looked up. "I didn't go to spend the day with a *man.*" She stared at her mother. "You know that. I went to see the lighthouse."

Her mother went to the window. "The keeper was there, and you were unchaperoned. That was improper for a girl your age. What will people think?"

"I don't care what people think," Faith said. "Why should I?" Out of the corner of her eye, Faith saw that Mr. Chesterfield took his hands out of his pockets and stood up straight. "You didn't care what people thought when you married Papa."

"Now that was totally uncalled for," Mr. Chesterfield growled.

"But it's the truth!" Faith turned to her mother. "Isn't it?"

Her mother turned pale, and then blushed red. "That was different," she said finally.

"Why was it different?"

Faith's mother's voice was like ice. "We will not talk about it any further," she said. "I want to know why you went to the lighthouse."

"I needed to see it," Faith said. "I needed to know . . ."

"Know what?" her mother asked.

"Whether he was taking care of it. Whether he was lighting the lamps." Faith spread her hands, palms up, in her lap.

"But you skipped school." Her mother turned back from the window. "You could be expelled for that."

Faith shrugged. "Let them expel me," she said. "I don't need to go to school."

"Now just one moment." Mr. Chesterfield stepped forward, but Faith's mother held up her hand, and he fell silent. Faith couldn't help being impressed.

"I know how you loved the lighthouse," her mother went on. "But skipping school? Going through the woods alone on a horse you can barely ride? Why couldn't you wait until a time we could all go together on the steamer?"

Faith gave a short laugh. "When would you go back on the steamer, Mama? How long would I have to wait?" Her mother's gaze flickered down and then up again, and Faith swallowed hard to keep back the tears burning behind her eyes. "If I wait for you, I'll never get back to the lighthouse."

Faith's mother walked to the window and back to the center of the room again. "The place holds painful memories," she said. "Can't you see that? It reminds me of your father. I can't bear to be there."

"And I can't bear not to be," Faith said. She began pacing around the small room, as if by moving she might find a crack, a way out of the dilemma.

"Is he taking care of it?" It was Mr. Chesterfield who spoke.

Faith stopped. "I beg your pardon?"

"Is the keeper taking care of the lighthouse?" Mr. Chesterfield stroked his chin. "Is he lighting the lamps?"

Faith turned to face him. "Yes," she said. "As a matter of fact, he is."

Mr. Chesterfield nodded. "Then you accomplished your purpose, young lady. The lighthouse is in good hands. You need not concern yourself with it again." He walked to the table and picked up the flute.

"But the walkway still hasn't been fixed," Faith said. "The keeper said he'd asked for the materials, but they haven't come yet."

Mr. Chesterfield sighed. "This is not your affair," he said. "Please leave the management of the lighthouse to me."

"But if the walkway's not fixed, it will never last through the season. The first big storm will break it in two."

"It's only September," Mr. Chesterfield said. "There's plenty of time before the storms hit. Please don't trouble yourself about it anymore."

"But, Mr. Chesterfield . . ."

He interrupted her. "I'll hear no more about it," he said. "I'll speak to the school authorities. You will be excused from punishment. This time." He put the flute back down on the table.

Faith wanted to scream. He wasn't listening to her at all. He was putting all the sailors on the lake in danger. For nothing. "You don't understand anything," she said.

"I would rather be whipped than have your help."

"Faith!" her mother stepped forward, hand over her mouth.

Mr. Chesterfield's face turned red, and his brows clamped down into a dark frown. He turned to Faith's mother. "This is exactly what I mean, Elizabeth. This kind of behavior must be nipped in the bud."

Faith's mother grabbed Faith by the arm. "I will have no rudeness," she said. Her voice trembled, but her hand gripped Faith's arm so hard it hurt. "Apologize to Mr. Chesterfield at once."

Faith looked at her mother; their eyes were on a level. "I will apologize," she said, "if he will apologize for trying to take the place of my father."

Mr. Chesterfield coughed. "I was not taking the place of your father. But someone must take charge of you."

"Why?" she asked. "I'm perfectly capable of taking charge of myself." She pulled her arm from her mother's grasp.

Mr. Chesterfield leaned a hand on the fireplace mantle. "Elizabeth, this is what happens when young girls are given too much freedom. They start thinking they can do anything they like." He turned to Faith. "Just because you successfully kept the lighthouse after your father died doesn't mean you are capable of making your own decisions."

"What does it mean, then?" Faith asked. "What does it mean that I made all kinds of decisions for that time? That my mother trusted me? That I did a man's job?" Her hands were shaking, and she gripped the back of the chair she was standing next to.

"It means . . ." Mr. Chesterfield took a breath and then let it out. "It means nothing. You must obey your mother."

"I have not said I would not obey my mother," Faith said. "Only that I will not obey you."

She turned to her mother, remembering the pride with which she'd told Nathaniel Kent that Faith was the keeper. "Does it mean nothing, Mama," she asked, "that I kept the light for all that time?"

Faith's mother was pale. She looked at Faith, and then at Mr. Chesterfield. Faith could see her lips tremble slightly. She looked back at Faith and cleared her throat. "You're a strong young woman, Faith," she said. "Stronger than I am, I think." She glanced at Mr. Chesterfield. "I think you discovered that after your father died, and you were left alone to tend the light. You did it well. I think that must mean something."

Faith felt a knot tight inside her chest begin to unwind just the slightest little bit.

Mr. Chesterfield opened his mouth to speak, but Faith's mother shook her head. Tears gathered in her eyes. "But I also think Harlan is right. I've been too lenient with you. At the lighthouse your father and I allowed you to run wild, but I thought when we moved to town you'd settle down." She shook her head, and the sad look in her eyes made Faith want to cry out. "I've tried so hard, Faith, but I haven't been able to teach you anything. I don't know how to make you see that you must learn to take your place as a woman in society."

Faith closed her eyes. The knot had tightened again. "It's not your fault," she whispered. She could no longer stop the tears. "I just can't do it."

"You haven't even tried." Her mother held out her hands to Faith. "Please?"

Faith looked at her mother's hands. She wanted so much to just grab them tight and hold on. But if she did, she would lose herself. She would lose the lighthouse. She had promised her father's memory one thing. Could she promise her mother another? Slowly she reached out and clasped her mother's slim white fingers. "I'll try, Mama," she said. A dark cloud began to settle around her heart. "I promise."

eleven

"Faith," Willy said, "Mama never said you couldn't ride Lady." They were standing at the corner of Water Street, under a huge maple tree with red-gold leaves, trying to decide whether to go home after school or over to Cassie's.

"I can't." Faith was nearly crying. "You don't understand. I promised."

"But what's one little ride?" Cassie put her hands on her hips. "I bet your mother would ride out with Mr. Chesterfield."

"But not in men's clothes," Faith pointed out.

"So, ride in your skirt," Cassie said. "It's such a perfect day. We could go out to the lighthouse path. There's plenty of time before supper. Maybe we could even . . ."

"No." Faith clenched her hands into fists. "That's the one place I can't go." She saw Cassie and Willy exchange a glance. "You don't need to look at each other that way. I've got to at least try to do what Mama wants."

Willy sighed. "You're no fun anymore," he said, scuffing his feet in the dirt. "I wish things could be the way they used to be."

"Well, I wish they could, too," Faith said. "But they can't." She turned to Cassie. "I'll talk to Mama. Maybe it would still be all right, as long as we don't go near the bluff path."

Cassie shrugged her shoulders and started off toward

her house. Faith watched her a moment, wondering if Cassie would still want to be her friend if Faith became the kind of woman her mother wanted.

She sighed. "Come on, Willy," she said. "It can't be helped." She took his hand and headed up the street.

But when they walked in the door, the first thing they saw was their mother's enormous traveling trunk sitting open in the middle of the small parlor.

"Where are you going?" Faith cried, throwing her cloak and bonnet down on the sofa.

Willy immediately climbed inside the trunk. "I'm going, too," he said. When he sat down, his eyes barely peeked over the top.

"Willy!" Their mother came in carrying a pile of towels. Her best dress was hanging over her arm. "Get out of there this instant. And Faith, hang up your things and help me fold this dress." She shook her head. "It never has packed well. It'll be full of wrinkles."

"But where are you going?" Faith helped her brother out of the trunk. "Go get us some cookies," she whispered, and Willy scampered off to the kitchen. She grabbed the hem of the dress, helping her mother to stretch it out flat. "Are we going, too?"

Her mother's shoulders drooped. "I wish you could," she said, giving the dress a slight shake and handing it to Faith. "But you can't. The land has finally sold, and I must go to Munising for the closing."

"How long will you be gone?" Faith folded the dress at the waist and waited while her mother spread a large piece of stiff paper in the trunk. Faith carefully laid the dress on top of the paper, and covered it with another piece.

Her mother sank down on the sofa. "I sail tomorrow on the *Mary*," she said. "I'll be gone a week if the weather holds." She reached behind her and pulled out Faith's bonnet, bent and creased. "I told you to hang this up. Now it's ruined."

Faith sighed. "I'm sorry, Mama." She took the bonnet and tried to reshape the brim. She went to hang her cloak up in the hall. "I can't even remember to hang up this stupid bonnet," she mumbled.

When she came back, her mother was lining the towels up in the trunk beside the dress. "Mama," she said, suddenly getting an idea. "Let me go with you."

"Don't be foolish, Faith," her mother said, straightening up. "You have school. And I need you to stay here and take care of Willy."

"I could come, too." Willy danced into the parlor and handed Faith one of the sugar cookies they'd made the day before. "I'd be good. I promise." He sat down on a chair and swung his legs back and forth. "You wouldn't even know I was there."

Their mother sighed. "We don't have the money for three tickets," she said. "Remember?"

"Do we have enough money for two tickets?" Faith leaned on the arm of Willy's chair and ran her fingers down a fold of her skirt. "I bet Cassie and her mam would take Willy for a week," she said. "And Cassie would check on the house, too. I know she would."

"But . . ." Willy opened his mouth to object, and Faith popped the last bite of her cookie into it.

"And you could ride Lady every day," she said.

"Every day?" Willy said through the mouthful of cookie. His eyes sparkled.

Faith's mother looked out the window, and Faith could tell she was considering it. "It would be such fun, Mama, she said. "Just you and me on an adventure." She paused. "You could teach me the proper way to go traveling."

"Well," her mother said. "Why don't you ask Cassie if

Willy could stay there for a while. We couldn't be sure when we'd be back. And you'd have to get your school-work."

Willy jumped up. "I'll ask about riding Lady," he said, running to the door. He opened it, and then came running back. "Mr. Chesterfield! His carriage is stopping outside."

"He's coming here?" Faith felt the now familiar tight-ness in her chest as her mother patted her hair and tugged at her skirt. "Now?"

Willy nodded. "Should I let him in?"

"Of course," said their mother, laughing. She went to the door and stood waiting.

Mr. Chesterfield took off his hat and gloves and placed them on the bench by the mirror. "I came as soon as I heard," he said.

Faith's mother made a face. "It won't take long," she said. "I can sail tomorrow and be back in a week if we have good weather." She took Mr. Chesterfield's arm and led him into the sitting room. "As you can see, I'm almost packed."

"I'm going to stay with Cassie." Willy skipped around the trunk. "And ride Lady every day. And Faith is going to Munising with Mama."

"That's quite unnecessary, Elizabeth." Mr. Chesterfield sat down in the big brown chair that used to be Faith's father's favorite. It was the only piece of furniture they'd brought back from the lighthouse. "That's why I came. I have to go to Munising, anyway, to see about materials for the new walkway." He gave a sideways glance at Faith. "I can escort you."

The room became suddenly silent. It's happening again, Faith thought. He's interfering where he's not want-ed. She stepped back and sat down on the window seat. Willy came over and climbed up beside her. "There's no reason you need to do this," she said, squeezing her hands together in her lap. "The trip to Munising won't be a problem for us."

"I believe your mother will be the judge of that," Mr. Chesterfield said. He looked at Faith's mother. "Are you sure you want her to miss that much school, Elizabeth?"

"I'm going to take my schoolwork with me," Faith put in quickly. "I was on my way to the teacher's house to see about it when you came."

Faith's mother smiled at Faith. "Harlan, I think Faith is right," she said. "We were looking forward to going on this journey together." She looked at Mr. Chesterfield. "Perhaps we can also see about the materials for the walkway, if you'll let us know who to talk to."

Faith's heart suddenly felt like it might explode with happiness. Her mother was choosing to go on an adventure with her.

Mr. Chesterfield looked at Faith's mother. "Elizabeth, are you sure you're doing the right thing?"

She nodded. "I'm sure. If Cassie is willing to take care of Willy and check on the house, we'll leave tomorrow afternoon."

Willy leaped up off the window seat. "Yippee! Let's go ask Cassie." He pulled Faith to her feet.

"Just a moment, please." Mr. Chesterfield reached into his pocket and took out a notebook. He smiled at Faith's mother. "Here's what I was planning to get for the walkway," he said, scribbling with a pencil on a blank page. "Talk to a Mr. Henson at the lumberyard on the edge of town." He turned to Faith. "The materials will be shipped on the same schooner you'll be coming home on, and the walkway will be repaired before the end of October, just as it should be."

Faith's heart was beating so loud, she could hardly hear

anything else. But for her mother's sake, she tried to remember her manners. "Thank you," she said, smiling at him. "I hope that will be soon enough."

Mr. Chesterfield nodded. "It will, Faith. I'm sure of it."

Cassie said she'd be delighted to watch Willy for the week, and promised him a ride on the mare every day after school. Faith collected her schoolwork from the teacher, and packed her clothes in the same trunk that held her mother's things.

But that night, Faith was awakened by the sound of Willy coughing in the next room. She slipped on her wrapper and went to him. "I thought I heard a seal barking in here," she said, looking at his grim little face framed by the huge white pillow.

"I'll have to have a mustard plaster, won't I?" he whispered hoarsely, scrubbing tears off his wet cheeks.

"I'm afraid so," she said. She sat down on the edge of his bed and tried not to let her own disappointment show in her face. Mama would never leave him alone with a cough like that—it was the way the pneumonia had started last spring.

But Willy knew their mother's ways as well as Faith did. "I'm not going to get to stay with Cassie, am I?" he said, his lower lip quivering.

Faith gave him a hug. "We couldn't leave you while you're sick," she said, smoothing his hair back from his face. His forehead felt hot and dry, and his eyes glittered with fever.

At that moment, Faith's mother appeared at the doorway with the box of mustard and a warm wet cloth. "I heard you coughing," she said, coming into the room. "I know how you hate this, but . . ."

Willy sighed. He sat up and unbuttoned his nightshirt.

"I might as well get it over with," he said. "Do you think I'll be all better in the morning?"

"We'll see," she said, motioning Faith to let her sit down on the bed. "Maybe you will." But the look she gave Faith told her there would be no adventure to Munising, at least not this week.

In the morning, knowing the plans for Munising were off, Faith fixed her own breakfast and gathered her things for school.

Her mother came down the stairs as she was fastening her cape. "Faith, do you think you can stay here this week and take care of Willy? You've already got your school-work."

Faith stared at her. "You're still going? How can you?"

Faith's mother sighed, and Faith could see the lines of worry around her eyes. "I have no other choice. I must sell the land this fall. We need the money badly—we owe almost every tradesman in town. We couldn't even pay the doctor. And with winter coming on . . ." She looked at Faith. "You know about winter storms on the lake. I'd be afraid to risk passage to Munising much later than this."

She handed Faith a letter. "I want you to go see Mr. Chesterfield. Perhaps he can go to Munising with me after all."

Faith took the letter, wishing Mr. Chesterfield didn't exist at all. "Mama," she said. "I could go. I know I could."

Faith's mother shook her head. "Of course you can't go to Munising by yourself. You're only a child."

"I'm not a child, Mama. I'm almost a grown woman." She tied her bonnet strings and drew her cloak over her shoulders. "I tended the lighthouse all that time. I know I could . . ."

But her mother's mouth was firm. "Please, let's not

start with that again, Faith. Go see Harlan, and then come right back here." She opened the door and ushered Faith out into the foggy air.

Mr. Chesterfield agreed with Faith's mother: It would be most improper for Faith to go to Munising by herself. "I admire your determination," he said, standing up behind the dark walnut desk in his office, "but it must be your mother who signs the contract. And I'd planned to go to Munising myself, as I told your mother. I would be delighted to accompany her." He pulled on the fine gold chain hanging from his waistcoat, and his pocket watch slid into his hand. "Now you'd better hurry back. I'll stop by later this morning to see about our tickets."

Faith's feet echoed on the board sidewalk as she headed toward the house on Water Street. The fog was lifting, and the sun was beginning to warm the chilly morning air. The sky was cloudless blue over her head. It would have been a wonderful beginning for the voyage to Munising, she thought gloomily. But instead she would be spending the entire day inside with Willy. It would be Mr. Chesterfield standing at the ship's rail with Mama, sniffing the wind and feeling the slow rocking of the waves on the lake.

twelve

The weather held warm and clear, and Faith tried to think about Willy and not her mother. His fever broke the next afternoon, and in a few days he was able to go back to school. He skipped along beside Cassie as he walked with the two girls the half mile to the schoolhouse. "Mama's coming home Friday," he said, "and Faith says we can have a picnic Saturday morning. Would you like to come?"

Cassie looked down at him, then over at Faith. "Could Lady come, too?"

"She can, can't she, Faith?" Willy tugged on Faith's hand. "Mama wouldn't mind. I know she wouldn't."

Would Mama approve? Faith wondered. What could be wrong with taking the mare on a picnic? Faith stepped carefully around a puddle in the road. "That's the trouble with me," she mused. "I don't have much idea of what's proper and what's not."

"The trouble with you is that you worry too much," Cassie said, shaking her head. "We'll wait and ask your mama, Willy." She grabbed Willy's hand, and they ran off down the street together, leaving Faith to walk alone.

It was as warm on Friday morning, and the sky was cloudless. Willy bounded out the door without his jacket when Cassie waved from the corner of Water Street.

But the minute Faith stepped outside, she noticed something different about the air. She stopped, sniffing the light breeze that barely set the leaves of the aspen trees in the front yard quivering.

"What's the matter?" Cassie called. She and Willy were waiting at the gate. "You look like an old hound dog." Willy laughed out loud.

Faith shook her head. "Something's different. Can you feel it?"

Cassie flung out her arms. "It's even warmer than yesterday," she said. "I think Indian summer will last till Christmas."

"It can't," Willy yelped. "I have a real sled this year." At the lighthouse he'd had only a bent-up old cookie sheet for sledding. But in the basement of the house on Water Street he'd found a sled. He'd hammered new slats over the broken ones and stood it by the back door, waiting for snow.

Faith turned around in a slow circle. There was nothing on the wind that she could smell, nothing she could see. She wondered if it would be the same at the lighthouse. "I think there's bad weather coming," she said.

Cassie looked around at the bright blue sky and laughed. "You're only worried about your mother," she said, nudging Faith with an elbow.

Even Willy eyed her doubtfully. "Today, Faith?" he said, his still pale face falling into lines of disappointment. "Mama comes today. And tomorrow is our picnic."

"Well," she said, "maybe it'll be even nicer tomorrow." She looked around. There was something in the very warmth of the morning that seemed unnatural for the end of September. But she shrugged off the prickles of feeling that made her scalp tingle, and followed the others to school.

In the middle of her morning history class, Faith suddenly realized she was squinting to see the letters in her textbook. She glanced up. The window was across the room from her desk, but the patch of sky she could see was gray. She shifted in her seat, wondering how hard the wind was blowing now, and an image of the angry face of Lake Superior floated in the back of her vision.

As if in answer to her question, one of the shutters banged against the window. Faith jumped, and dropped her pencil.

Cassie touched her on the shoulder and pointed silently to the window. "You were right," she mouthed.

Faith nodded, taking no pleasure in it. She reached out with the toe of her shoe and pulled the pencil back to her chair. Now it would be days before her mother returned, because surely the *Mary* would wait in Munising for better weather.

The shutter banged again. "Ben?" Miss Ward, the teacher, tapped with her pointer. "Could you go refasten that shutter, please?"

"Yes, ma'am," he said, unfolding his great length from under the desk. He strode out of the classroom, and soon they heard him struggling with the heavy shutter. In a moment he was back. "Hook's pulled clean out of the wall," he said. "I'll need a hammer to fix it." He looked around the room. "It's getting nasty out there."

Though he'd been speaking to everyone, Faith felt he was talking only to her. "Storm?" she asked him, her heart beginning to thump wildly.

He took the hammer the teacher handed him. "Seems like," he said. "Them clouds look about as dark as I've ever seen." He tested the weight of the hammer in his hand and went to fix the shutter.

Faith suddenly found herself standing by her desk. She *had* to get outside.

"Yes, Faith?" Miss Ward looked at her, eyebrows raised.

"Nothing, ma'am." Faith sat down quickly. But first she

glanced again out the window. The trees were whipping frantically in the wind, and bright leaves flew thick as snow.

The rest of the morning was agony. Faith could hear the wind whistling in the crack of the window and crying around the corners of the schoolhouse. Every now and then a spatter of rain pelted the windowpanes. It sounded like someone was throwing gravel at the glass.

Storms come from the west, she kept telling herself, so Munising would have been hit first. "They must be safe in Munising," she whispered. But her stomach felt as if she'd swallowed a stone.

At lunch, Faith grabbed her pail and, dodging around the other students, ran for the front door. She passed Cassie, who was heading for the classroom.

"You're not going to eat outside, are you?" Cassie called to her.

"I've got to see what's happening," Faith shouted. "I'll be right back."

It was as though the warm, quiet morning had never existed. The temperature had dropped, turning the occasional sprinkle of rain to a light sleet. Black clouds blotted out the sun and covered the sky with gray cotton fog. The wind blew in great gusts, bending some of the slender aspens in front of the school almost double in its fury. Leaves, scraps of paper, flecks of wood and dirt, even a man's tall hat, were all skipping and tumbling down the street together.

Stronger than ever came the image of the lake, waves churning in all directions, crashing against each other and up onto the sand. Faith imagined seagulls trying to fly against the wind, held in place in the air by an invisible hand, and the geysers of foam spraying up as the waves hit the half-submerged boulders stretching out into the lake from the lighthouse.

And then, like a thunderclap, she realized that this storm was coming up from the east. Most likely the *Mary* started out in the fine weather of last night and this morning. The captain might have no idea of the storm raging here. And her mother would be on board.

Faith closed her eyes. This storm would surely rip the temporary boards from the walkway and pull down the broken railing. The keeper should be going out to the beacon now, before the walkway cracked, she thought. He could take extra oil, and keep the beacon lit through the storm. But would he think of it?

Faith spun around. She had to get to the lighthouse before it was too late. She started back into the schoolhouse to look for Cassie, but then she remembered her promise. If she skipped school again, her mother would never believe she was trying to be a proper lady. Especially now that she was left alone and in charge of Willy.

But if she didn't go, if the beacon didn't get lit, her mother might die in a shipwreck. She took a step into the schoolhouse, and then stopped again. Maybe the keeper was lighting the lamps at this very moment, she told herself. Maybe she wasn't needed at the lighthouse.

The wind tore at her, as if trying to pull her out of the building and down the street. In her mind she saw the ship getting closer and closer to the submerged rocks off the shore. It wasn't real, she told herself sternly. The *Mary* would still be far down the coast.

But then she realized that the image she saw wasn't the *Mary*. It was the *Alice Rutherford* she was remembering, the ship her father had died trying to rescue. Would her mother die in this storm if Faith didn't get there to help the keeper? Would she have the deaths of both her father and her mother on her head?

And suddenly it was no longer a question. She'd rather lose her mother's trust than her life. "I'm sorry, Mama," she whispered. "I have to do this. Even if you can't ever forgive me, I have to."

"Cassie," she called as she ran into the classroom. Heads jerked up, and eyes stared at her for the outburst, but she didn't care. "Come here." She grabbed Cassie by the arm and almost dragged her out of the room.

"I've got to borrow Lady," she said as they huddled in a corner of the hallway. I've got to get to the lighthouse."

Cassie stared at her. "Now?" She shook her head. "It's going to storm. And besides, Nat will keep the light lit. I know he will."

Faith ground her teeth and tried to be patient. "The walkway will go to bits with these waves," she said. "I've got to get there before it gets too bad. I've got to tell him the only thing he can do is take extra oil and spend the night in the lighthouse."

Cassie pulled on a lock of her hair that had fallen into her eyes. "Maybe he'll think of that," she said, looking out the window at the worsening storm.

"But what if he doesn't?" Faith asked. "What if the *Mary* started out this morning?" Her voice trembled. "My mother's on that schooner."

Cassie nodded, making up her mind. "My riding clothes are in the stable." She gave Faith a hug. "I'll bring Willy home with me after school."

Faith rushed to the front door, past Miss Ward, who was coming out of a room at the end of the hall. "Faith! What is happening?" she called.

But there was no time to explain, and Faith had no intention of being stopped, now that she'd made up her mind. She raced by the teacher, pulled hard on the big front doorknob, and she was out in the storm.

thirteen

The wind at her back pushed her down the street as though it understood the hurry. Yet Faith felt like she was running in a sea of molasses. Each step seemed painfully slow. When she finally reached her house, she didn't stop, but cut through the yard and under the pines to Cassie's house.

The stable was warm and quiet after the cold wind outside. Lady pricked up her ears and gave a soft whinny as Faith slammed the stable door shut and began to struggle out of her dress and petticoats. She left them in a pile of clean straw, pulled on the wool pants, shirt, and jacket Cassie always rode in, and went to get the tack.

She grabbed a carrot from the barrel. "Here, Lady," she said, and let the horse munch as she slapped the blanket and saddle onto her back. She buckled the cinch. "Is that tight enough?" she asked, wishing the mare could answer. It would be awful if the saddle fell off halfway to the lighthouse.

She slid the bridle bit into Lady's mouth, and adjusted the straps around her ears. Lady looked longingly at the carrot barrel, but Faith grabbed the reins and pulled her past it, out into the storm. "There's no time, Lady girl," she said, swinging herself up into the saddle. "Maybe the keeper will have something for you to eat." She tapped Lady's sides with her heels, and the mare, uncomplaining as usual, took off at a brisk trot.

The wind was blowing even harder than before. The trees looked as if they were bowing to some unseen king. An occasional splatter of sleet pelted Faith's shoulders and Lady's rump. Now and then a leaf or a stick whipped by. But Faith kept a tight hand on the reins. Fortunately the wind was at her back; she wasn't sure she could force even Lady to move into the gale.

Parts of the path along the bluff were protected by the trees, and Lady's footsteps seemed sure but slow. Faith clucked to her, "Come on, girl. We've got to go faster than this." Lady trotted for a moment, then settled back into a walk as the path came out of the huge pines and ran along the very edge of the cliff top.

The lake was as gray and angry as she'd imagined. The water churned like some huge boiling cauldron. Waves crashed every which way, sending white foam bubbling into the air. There were no gulls that she could see—they were wisely seeking shelter inland. Faith knew the walkway wouldn't last long under the pressure of those waves. She had to go faster.

The path turned back under the trees, and Faith urged Lady to a trot. "It'll be too late," she shouted over the roar of the storm. She kicked Lady's flanks. The mare broke into a canter, and Faith bent low over her neck. "Come on, girl," she whispered. She listened to the thud of Lady's hooves on the path, willing them on, faster and faster.

A slight skip in the rocking rhythm caused Faith to look up, and what she saw made her heart seem to stop. The path ended abruptly about six feet ahead. It was the sandy place Lady had refused to cross before. The underpinnings of the cliff had crumbled, leaving a four-foot gap in the trail.

Before she had time to think what to do, she felt Lady's

muscles bulge. She grabbed tight to the saddle, and in a heartbeat they were flying over the gap, not even a foot from the edge of the cliff. Faith squeezed her eyes shut and hoped she wouldn't fall off when they landed.

She opened her eyes as Lady cleared the gap with room to spare, and settled back into a canter. Now Faith could see the lighthouse, looking almost as gray as the water surrounding it. She couldn't tell if the walkway was still intact, but she could see that the windows were dark. She scanned the horizon for schooners. Mercifully, the lake was empty.

"Please let them have stayed in Munising," she prayed. She tried to envision the schooner sitting safe and still in the harbor, but the only image that came to her mind was that of the ship out on the open water, battling the wind and waves. She shook the picture away.

Lady's coat was dark with water and sweat, and Faith could feel her sides heaving. "Just a little further, girl," she whispered. They were beginning the series of switchbacks that would take them to the beach. She felt Lady slow to a walk and brace with her forelegs. Faith leaned back in the saddle and gritted her teeth. They couldn't go faster than a walk here; if Lady slipped, they'd go down for sure.

As though she understood the hurry, when they reached the bottom Lady put her head down and broke into a dead gallop, heading for the lighthouse. Clods of wet sand flew from her hooves as she ran. Faith put her head on the horse's neck and closed her eyes.

Of her own accord, Lady stopped at the boathouse, just where she'd waited for Faith that other afternoon. Faith looked around. She could see only one railing on the walkway, but she couldn't tell about the planks since the waves kept them completely underwater. The keeper was nowhere to be seen. She slid to the ground and leaned against Lady's strong side, exhausted by the ride and almost as out of breath as the horse. And her work had barely begun.

She uncinched the saddle and pulled it off Lady's back. There wasn't time to brush her down, but Faith couldn't simply leave her here unattended. She ran to the boathouse and flung open the door. The lifeboat was suspended from ropes, and Faith reached in for the bucket she knew was kept in the bow.

Filling the bucket from the lake, Faith was on her way back to Lady when the keeper came charging around the corner of the boathouse. He saw Faith and Lady and stopped dead.

"What are *you* doing here?" His shout startled Lady, who shied and made a move to run. But the keeper was close enough to grab the reins. "Whoa, girl," he said, his voice turning silky. "You're too tired to bolt." He reached slowly to pat Lady's neck and her trembling forelegs.

"You've run this horse hard, Miss Sutton." He sounded angry. "What on earth do you think you're doing?"

Faith put the bucket down in front of Lady, who bent immediately to drink. "Is the walkway holding?" She had to shout to be heard over the crash of waves on the beach. "We've got to get out to the tower now, before it breaks up." She grabbed the reins from the keeper and began wrapping them around the lantern post.

The keeper took a quick glance around. "You may know a lot about lighthouses, Miss Sutton," he said, "but you don't know much about horses. She can't stay out in the storm." He pushed Faith's hands away and took Lady's reins, leading her into the boathouse.

Without a word, Faith grabbed up the bucket and followed the keeper. There was plenty of room beside the lifeboat, and Faith put the bucket down on the dirt floor where Lady could reach it easily.

KEEPER of the LIGHT

"Now if you'll please explain . . . ," the keeper began.

"There's no time." Faith interrupted him. "If we each get two cans of oil from the barrel, it should be enough to last." She tried to duck around him.

"What are you raving about?" the keeper shouted, planting himself firmly in the doorway. "It's not close to evening yet." He glanced out the dirty window. "This storm may play itself out by then."

Faith stared at him. "This storm," she said, almost growling, "will probably last two days. If you don't get to the tower now, you won't be able to get there at all. The waves have already taken one railing, and who knows about the planks." She put her hand on his arm. "If you're not going to help, then stand out of my way."

At the mention of the broken railing, the keeper turned his head to look. She saw him swallow, and his mouth opened in surprise. It was obvious he hadn't even checked the walkway. He spun back to her, but stepped aside and followed her to the shed where the oil was kept.

Faith flung open the shed door. She grabbed an empty oilcan, filled it from the barrel, and handed it to the keeper. "This is why we keep so many empties," she said, filling another can for him.

The keeper swished the oil in the can. "Isn't this too cold?" he asked. "I've been warming it up before I fill the reservoir."

Faith filled two cans for herself. "We'll figure out a way to warm it when we get there," she said. "Maybe we can light a fire with some of the rags."

The wind was fierce, and the icy rain felt like knives on Faith's face. Every time she closed her eyes, all she saw was the *Mary*, tossing in the storm. She leaned into the wind and kept her eyes open.

"Can you tell if the planks are safe?" the keeper shouted

into Faith's ear as they reached the shore.

Faith watched the waves smashing into the rocks. "I don't think so," she yelled back. Before the keeper could object, Faith put her cans of oil down, grabbed the one good railing with both hands, and started to cross.

"Hey!" the keeper roared at her.

"I'm going to check," she called back over her shoulder. Step by step she pulled herself along, fighting the wind, fighting the waves. She was wet clear through, but she couldn't feel the cold at all, except in the pit of her stomach whenever she thought of the *Mary*. She would beat this storm yet.

But before she was halfway to the break, she knew the temporary planks were gone. She could feel it in the way the ones she stood on swayed and shifted under her feet.

She wanted to scream, but knew not to waste her energy. She glanced down. The hidden rocks were there, under the chaos of the waves. If she slipped now, no one could save her; she'd be beaten to death between rock and water. She began inching her way back, hoping the remaining planks would hold till she reached the shore.

fourteen

"We can't get there that way," Faith shouted to the keeper. He'd put his cans of oil down and reached for her hand as she stepped off the walkway. For an instant all she wanted to do when she got off those shifting planks was to sink down on the solid sand, and she was glad for the strength of the keeper's arm. She looked at his face; it was white with strain, and she found she felt sorry for him.

"I should have checked it earlier," he said, swallowing hard. He scanned the horizon. "Maybe there won't be any need . . . ," he said, his voice trailing off.

"The *Mary*'s due in Token Creek in a few hours," she said. She headed for the boathouse. "She sailed from Munising this morning. We've got to get the beacon lit."

"Surely they didn't start from Munising in this storm," the keeper shouted. He was following her.

"This storm came from the east," she said, not looking back. "And it came up fast." She reached the boathouse and flung open both the wide doors.

"What are you doing?" The keeper grabbed one of the doors, holding it closed with both hands. The wind roared in Faith's ears so loud, she could hardly hear him.

"I'm going over in the lifeboat," Faith screamed at him. "Open that door!" Inside the boathouse, the wind wasn't so loud. She could hear Lady's hooves shifting in the dirt and the creaking of the shed as the wind blew against it.

She reached to loosen the ropes that suspended the lifeboat from the beams of the shed, but the keeper caught her hand.

"It's impossible," he shouted.

"It can't be." Faith yanked her hand away and grabbed for the ropes. She untied one end, and the boat's bow bumped to the dirt. Lady, who'd been standing beside it, stepped nervously aside and whinnied.

The keeper grabbed Faith by the waist and pulled her away from the second rope. "The lifeboat will crack up on those rocks even faster than a schooner would," he said. "You'd never make it."

Faith struggled against him, but he was stronger than she was. He got his arms around her and dragged her away from the boat.

"Let me go," she shouted, beating on his shoulders. "My mother's coming home on the *Mary*. I *have* to get to the lighthouse."

And suddenly she was free. They stood in the boathouse staring at each other. "I won't let you risk it," the keeper said. He pointed out to the gray and angry lake. "Your mother has a better chance in the *Mary* than you do in the lifeboat. It would be suicide to try."

Faith looked out. Foam spewed into the air as the wind and waves hit the rocks. He was right. She'd be killed if she tried to take a boat out to the lighthouse. Like her father. She closed her eyes and leaned up against the lifeboat.

"The night the *Alice Rutherford* went down and your father drowned," the keeper said slowly, "was the beacon lit?"

Faith listened to the wind crying outside the shed. She looked away from the keeper. "No," she whispered, remembering the cold dread of the black and empty lighthouse windows that dark night. "I was supposed to light it, but the oil was sluggish. I didn't get it warm enough." She turned. "The lamp lit, but then it went out, and I couldn't get it going again in time."

She felt him shift from one foot to the other. "That's why it's so important," she said. "Don't you see? I let my father die. I can't let my mother die."

"You didn't let your father die," the keeper said. "He chose to take the lifeboat out. And besides, how do you know the *Alice Rutherford* wouldn't have wrecked, anyway? Even if you had gotten the lamp lit."

She looked up at him. That's what her mother said. And that nobody could have gotten the oil warm enough that night. And that the *Alice Rutherford* had no business even being out on the lake at all. She sighed. She knew all the reasons why it hadn't been her fault. "But I didn't get the beacon lit. And my father died."

The wind sounded louder than ever in the silence. He looked away from her, out to the lake. "But we can't get to the lighthouse," he said. "It's too late."

Faith went to the door. The sleet had stopped for a moment. "Maybe we could make another lighthouse," she said, a plan forming in her head. "Where are those cans of oil?"

"They're down on the beach," he said. "What do you mean, 'another lighthouse'?"

"Another light, anyway," she answered. She rummaged in a metal box her father had always kept in the bow of the lifeboat and pulled out some matches. "Get the oil. We're going to burn Willy's fort."

"What?"

"The fort," Faith repeated, impatient. "That pile of brambles down the beach."

The keeper nodded, understanding immediately. "I

wondered what that was," he said. He headed for the walkway.

Faith ran to the oil shed and filled two more cans. There was no telling how hard it would be to light a bonfire in this storm.

The outer branches of Willy's fort were covered with a thin layer of ice. But inside, the wood was still dry and brittle and soaked up the oil like a sponge.

"Now cover it all with oil," Faith told the keeper, and together they emptied all but one can on the wet wood. The wind was blowing steadily, and the sleet had started up again. Faith stared out into the darkness, but the fading light and the icy rain made it impossible to see even a hundred feet out over the water. If there was a ship out there, it was invisible in the storm.

"I hope this works," the keeper murmured. He cupped his hands around the match as Faith struck it on the box. It lit, but went out as she threw it onto the pile. The same thing happened with the second match.

"Damnation!" the keeper said, and then glanced up at Faith. "Sorry."

Faith waved her hand. "Don't be silly," she said. She crouched by the pile of branches. "Here. Help me block the wind."

The keeper squatted down beside her. Faith held the box as close to the pile as she could and struck another match. Quickly she tossed it into the middle of the fort, and with a sharp crackle, the inside branches caught.

"Get back!" The keeper pulled her away as the fire erupted from the center of the fort. Fed by oil and wind, the flames leaped up as if reaching to touch the black clouds, and Faith's hope grew with them.

She gripped the keeper's arm. "It's going to work," she cried. "They couldn't help but see that."

The flames lit the keeper's face. "It may not be a lighthouse beacon," he said, "but it'll tell them where the shore is, sure enough." He looked relieved.

"We have to keep it burning," Faith said. "You go that way, and I'll go this way. Get all the driftwood you can."

In ten minutes they were both back at the fire. Faith had an armload of driftwood kindling, and the keeper had the same, and he also dragged a huge tree limb behind him. They made a pile beside the bonfire.

"Shall we break this up," he asked, kicking the limb, "or just throw it on like this?"

"Break it up," Faith decided, going down on her knees in the sand. She looked up at the keeper. "I don't think I'll ever wear skirts again," she said. "Trousers are so much handier."

The keeper laughed. "For this kind of work," he said. "But it wouldn't be as much fun to dance with a woman if she were wearing trousers."

"And think of what Mr. Chesterfield would say," Faith said, giggling. "And my mother!" She looked up at the keeper, who schooled his features into a properly horrified expression, and then grinned down at Faith.

He's not so bad after all, she thought, turning to throw a branch on the fire.

Then, over the top of the flame, she thought she saw something out in the lake. She froze, blinking, squinting her eyes against the brightness of the fire. "Nat?" she whispered, standing slowly. "I saw something."

He stopped breaking up the limb. "Where?"

"Right there." Faith pointed. She stepped away from the fire, peering into the dusk. At that instant, the rain came pouring down in sheets, and the wind blew even more furiously. The waves came rolling across the beach, each one closer to the fire than the one before.

Faith waded out into the foaming surf, and the keeper came to stand beside her. "What did you see?" he asked.

"Something. It could have been a ship." Faith felt herself begin to shake all over. "It was out at the line of boulders."

Nat put both hands up to shield his eyes from the rain, but shook his head. "I can't see anything," he said. "This damnable storm is getting worse. The waves will douse the fire in another minute."

"It doesn't matter," Faith said, pointing. "Look."

It matched the vision she'd tried earlier to put out of her mind. Out at the edge of the rocks a shadowed shape battled the wind. The schooner's sails were gone, but Faith could see the deck and the three towering masts. The ship was rolling wildly, spinning this way and that in the crashing waves.

"Broke her steering gear," Nat said. They watched in silence as the ship fought her way to the shore.

But she was heading for the rocks. "The anchor! Throw out the anchor!" Faith ran through the waves, shouting to the ship even though no one on board could possibly hear her. But after a time its forward movement stopped.

Nat caught up to Faith. "The water's rising," he said. "We've got to get out of here."

"No," Faith said, brushing his outstretched hand aside. "We can't leave them. We'll get the lifeboat." She couldn't take her eyes off the storm-tossed schooner. If she did, it might disappear forever.

"Faith!" Nat took her by the shoulders and shook her. "The lifeboat will crack up on the rocks. That's what happened to your father. No one can survive in this surf."

"But we have to do something," she screamed at him. She could feel tears clogging her throat. She couldn't give up. She couldn't.

They stood watching a minute longer. The wild waves were up to their knees now, and only a strip of beach was left in front of the towering cliff side.

"I'm going for higher ground," Nat said. He turned and splashed away through the waves.

Faith was left alone. She waded back to the bonfire, where she rescued the remaining full can of oil from the water. If the ship's anchor held, there might be a chance, she thought. But if not, the schooner would be blown full onto the rocks. Faith found a small cleft in the cliff face where there was some protection from the wind. She was going to be ready, she thought, if there was even the smallest chance to help. Her mother would be furious to find her here, but that no longer mattered. She sat down and prepared to watch.

fifteen

Full dark came. Faith's hands and feet were numb with cold. She huddled out of the wind, grateful for her thick woolen jacket, but shivering uncontrollably all the same. It seemed there was nothing left in the world except the shrinking strip of sand beach she was sitting on, the stretch of angry water, and the schooner straining at her anchor.

The rain fell steadily, but the wind blew in gusts; sometimes it seemed to be trying to smash the ship against the rocks, and then it would quiet for a moment, as if gathering strength for another assault.

Faith tried to shut out the image of her mother as she must be on the ship, terrified and clinging to a rope somewhere to keep from being washed overboard. Maybe she was hurt already, or worse. Faith took deep breaths to quell the panic rising in her chest. Hysteria would be no help at all, she told herself sternly.

When she squinted she could just make out the shape of the schooner in the slanting rain. If only she could somehow communicate with the crew, Faith thought. It was impossible for them to hear her over the wind and crashing waves, but if they knew she was here, maybe she could do *something*.

She felt in the pocket of her jacket and found that the matches were still dry. She had pushed the last can of oil back as far as she could reach into the cleft to keep the water out of it. She might be able to light some kind of a torch. But what could she burn in all this wet? She looked toward the dark lighthouse, wishing without much hope that Nat would come with a lantern.

She struggled to her feet. Her legs were stiff and sore from sitting and from cold; she jumped up and down and stamped the sand to get the blood running back into her toes. Then with one eye on the rocking vessel, she began poking around at the base of the cliff. Perhaps she could find a stout branch or a piece of driftwood that was not too wet.

It took longer than she'd expected, but finally, under a thick pile of leaves and pine needles, she found two relatively dry pieces of driftwood and a partly rotted board about two feet long.

Faith carried the wood back to the cleft. She decided to try the board first; it might burn longer, and somehow it seemed like good luck to use this surviving piece of some ancient shipwreck to help save the *Mary*.

She faced the cliff, hunkering down to keep out of the wind and rain, and dipped the would-be torch in the oil. Then, leaning it up against the rock, she slid the matches out of her pocket and struck one. Over and over she scraped the match on the box. She could smell the acrid stench of phosphorus, and she even got a spark once, but the match wouldn't light.

"Damn," Faith whispered once and then felt her ears burning in spite of the cold. Her mother would be horrified if she heard her daughter swear, even under these circumstances. She threw the match away and got another one.

It must have been drier, for it flared at the first scratch. Faith brought it close to the wood, set the oil afire, and then held the torch under the sheltering overhang until the wood caught. She breathed in the odor of oil and burning wood as if it were perfume.

When it was burning fiercely, Faith swung the torch out into the rain. At first the glare nearly blinded her, but she lifted the torch up over her head, and then she could see again.

"I'm here," she screamed, splashing into the waves. "Can you see me?" She paced back and forth in the water, hoping the movement of the light would catch their attention. "Hey!" she shouted. "I'm here! I'll help you."

The torch began to sputter, and she waded back to the cleft. As soon as it was out of the rain, the flame blazed back, strong and bright. Faith picked up one of the pieces of driftwood and set it on end in the can of oil, getting ready for the next torch, and then turned back to the ship.

What she saw made her want to sing. A small bright ball of light was swinging back and forth on the deck. A lantern. They *had* seen her. She waved the torch back and forth, screaming at the top of her lungs. "Hey! Hey!" she called. "How can I help you?"

Her torch sputtered again, and went out. Faith ran to the oilcan and grabbed the waiting piece of driftwood. Frantically she struck a match, and the oil coating the dry wood caught immediately. She placed both the second piece of driftwood and the unburned end of the board in the oil.

She waded as far as she dared into the water, holding the torch high. Then, out of the corner of her eye she caught movement—it looked like a firefly wobbling down the beach toward her. She knew what it was: Nat was running with the lantern.

He stayed back on the sand. "Are you all right?" he called to her. "I heard you scream."

"Look," she said, pointing. "They know we're here."

The lantern on the ship was sweeping back and forth in a great arc, as if the person holding it were swinging it out at arm's length. And then, over the roar of the wind and the crashing waves, they heard a sound like an explosion.

The anchor line had snapped. Faith screamed, and the lantern light on the ship abruptly went out.

Nat was suddenly standing in the water beside her. They watched as the wind snatched at the ship's hull, whipping it broadside. To Faith it seemed as though the ship gave a giant leap and lurched up onto the rocks. "Oh no, oh no," she whimpered, grabbing Nat's arm. "She'll go to pieces."

"Not right away," Nat said, pulling her back out of the water.

"Now we've *got* to get the lifeboat," Faith said. She tried to hand the torch to him.

But Nat grabbed her wrist, instead. "Faith, listen," he screamed at her. "Why do you keep wanting to use the lifeboat? Do you want to kill yourself like your father?" He held up her hand, and the torch sputtered. "If you do, go right ahead." He let go of her arm. "But I don't see how that will help your mother."

Faith glared at him, but she went back to the oilcan. She plunged the torch into the oil, grabbed the other piece of driftwood, and lit it. There weren't very many matches left.

"From now on we have to light the new torch with the old one," she said, handing it to Nat, who had followed her back to the shelter of the cliff. "We need to save the matches."

He was looking at the *Mary*. She was listing badly, and Faith knew she was taking a pounding from the rocks. "Maybe they can float us a line," Nat said. "At least we could help hold her steady."

The ship was hardly more than a hundred feet away from shore, but the noise from the storm made communication impossible. Faith stood in the water and watched, helpless, as the ship was flung from side to side by the wind and waves. She could feel the cold water sucking at her feet and ankles as the waves drew back and then washed shoreward.

"Look." Nat grabbed her arm and pointed. "Something's happening." Something *was* happening. Light had appeared again on deck, two lanterns this time. "I bet they *are* sending us a line."

Nat was already moving out, scanning the waves. Faith went in the opposite direction as far as she dared. She had to brace herself as each wave thundered toward the shore. It was so dark, she was afraid she'd never see anything in the water.

Her heart thumped as she caught sight of something white, but it was just the foam of whitecaps breaking. How long would it take to float the line in, she wondered, if that was indeed what they were doing.

She glanced over at Nat, and then back to the lake. A white flash at the corner of her eye made her turn her head. She could see nothing. She stared at the place—there it was again, a white speck that floated up on the swell and then disappeared.

"There." Faith called to Nat without taking her eyes from the place she last saw it. "Right there."

Nat came splashing over. "Where?"

She pointed as a small white something rose up in the dark and then disappeared.

"It's just waves cresting," Nat said, staring.

"No," she said. "Whitecaps dissolve. This stays steady. Just watch."

There it was again, a little closer this time. "See? They've tied a line to a life preserver. You were right!" She grabbed the keeper's sleeve.

Faith stepped two paces farther into the lake and felt

the sand give beneath her feet. "Nat?" she shouted, reaching out. He grabbed her hand and pulled her back.

"We're about as far out as we dare," he said. "We'll just have to wait till it comes to us."

Faith clenched her fists, and the blood pounded in her head. Each time the waves swelled she could see the life preserver. It was getting closer inch by inch, and behind it was the form of the rolling schooner, tossing this way and that on the rocks.

It seemed like hours until Nat was reaching for the life preserver. Faith grabbed it with both hands, and together they dragged it toward the beach. It had looked so small floating out in the lake, but in reality it was almost three feet across. Tied to it was a light line.

"Wave the torch," Faith cried once they had the line untied. "We can pull the mooring rope in."

Nat walked back to the cleft, doused the torch, and put the wood back into the oilcan, while Faith started hauling in the line. Big as it was, the life preserver could never have kept the heavy mooring line afloat, so the sailors had tied a light line to the life preserver, and the mooring line, the hawser, would be tied to that.

After what seemed like forever, Faith's wet fingers finally gripped the hawser; it was thicker than her wrist, and hummed and bucked in her hands like a living thing. "We'll never be able to hold it," she said to Nat. "We've got to brace it around something."

"A tree," Nat suggested. But there were no trees on the beach—the nearest ones were at the top of the cliff, fifty feet above them.

They both looked up. "There's no way we could get the line up there," Nat said. "Not in the dark."

"What about the rock?" Faith said. "The one we sat on when I showed you the knots."

Nat nodded. "It's worth a try," he said.

The rock Faith had always used for a bench when she watched the lake was on higher ground. They dragged the line back to it.

"Get the rope down as close to the ground as you can," Nat said as they reached the boulder. "How deep is this thing buried, anyway?"

"It's deep," Faith said. She looked out at the *Mary*; the schooner seemed to be lying almost horizontal in the water, and a lump came into Faith's throat. "My father said it reaches to China."

Nat grunted. "Let's hope he was right," he said. He dragged the line out straight and then, bracing it against the boulder, he began to pull it tight. "Is it holding?"

Faith checked it. "I think so." She wedged the rope into a slight indentation in the rock's side. Please let this work, she prayed silently, and she moved to the other side of the rock to help Nat pull.

They leaned together against the weight of the rope, stretched it tight, and then pulled again.

"Harder," Nat growled. He dug his heels into the sand, and Faith moved her hands farther up on the rope. Then Faith held the line, and Nat moved his hands. Inch by inch they tightened it until with a mighty twang they could hear above the wind, the rope lifted out of the water.

"Not enough," Nat shouted. "Now we've got to get it tighter."

Faith could see the *Mary*; waves were splashing up higher than the deck, and she was tossing as much as ever. But, slowly, as they tightened the line, the ship quieted. The tension from the rope was holding her just steady enough to stop the worst of the pounding.

"Now wrap it around again," Faith said, and Nat did. They coiled it twice more around the boulder, and then worked the end under one of the wrapped coils to hold it. Faith's hands were scratched and blistered from holding the prickly rope, and it was a relief to be able to let go.

"What time do you suppose it is?" Faith asked, knowing they could do nothing more for the ailing ship until morning.

"I could go see," Nat said.

"Let me," Faith said. "I need to warm up." She huffed on her chapped fingers, and her breath filled the air like smoke.

Nat nodded. "I think there are coals in the cookstove and enough coffee in the pot for two cups. Would you bring me one? And a baked potato? They're in a bowl on the warming shelf. Eat one yourself, too."

Faith nodded. She looked once more at the ship, sitting quiet now. There was a lantern glowing at the prow and another at the stern. They were keeping watch on the ship. She crossed the sand to the house, realizing suddenly that she was trusting Nat to watch from shore while she was in the house. She turned to see him sitting on the boulder with the end of the rope in his lap—a lifeline to the ship.

Somehow she'd expected the house to be different with Nat living there. But the kerosene lamp was in its same place on the chest, and as she lit it with the matches they always kept there, she looked around to find the kitchen strangely unchanged. They'd left most of the furniture, of course, since it belonged to whatever keeper was living there at the time. And Nat had not moved anything.

She added a few pieces of kindling to the firebox and blew on the coals until flames started licking up. Then she added two more sticks, shut the firebox door, and put the coffee on to heat.

She lifted the lamp and went to look in the other rooms. One stuffed chair was closer to the fireplace in the living room, and Nat's spindly legged table and an elaborate kerosene lamp with a tasseled shade were sitting next to it. There was a book there; Faith could read *Robinson Crusoe* on the spine, and she wondered if Nat felt he had a lot in common with the marooned sailor.

Should she look into his bedroom? Her mother would greatly disapprove, but Faith did it, anyway. Nat had strung a clothesline there, and two pairs of long underwear and some socks were hanging to dry. So he washed his own laundry, she thought.

The house was surprisingly clean and neat; Nat was a careful housekeeper. Faith grinned; her mother would be impressed. She wondered whether he'd still cook and clean and do laundry when he got married.

Probably not, she decided, putting the lamp back on the chest. The old clock on the kitchen shelf said twelve-fifteen. Only twelve hours had passed since she'd left school. It seemed like much longer. She wondered what Cassie had told the teacher about her absence. Maybe they'd whip her this time. She sighed and tried not to think about how disappointed her mother would be.

She retrieved two mugs from the china cupboard in the kitchen, set them on the stove, and filled them with steaming coffee. She found a pile of clean dishcloths in a drawer and used one to wrap two baked potatoes. She'd noticed a big oilcloth neatly folded on the chest beside the lamp; she tucked it under her arm along with the package of potatoes, picked up a cup in each hand, and went back out into the storm.

The *Mary* was riding relatively quiet in the water, and Nat was still sitting on the boulder. He took the cups from her and swallowed a large gulp of coffee. "Still hot," he said, grimacing. "Thanks."

She nodded and put the potatoes down on the boulder.

"I brought this," she said, unfolding the oilcloth. "I thought we could make it into a kind of tent. If you sit on one end and I sit on the other, I don't think it'll flap too badly in the wind."

She sat down beside him, and they pulled the cloth up over their heads. It made a kind of cave, falling down to cover their backs and heads, but open to the lake so they could see the schooner. The rain spattered on the oilcloth, louder with each gust of wind. Faith warmed her hands on the coffee mug and sipped the bitter liquid.

"Would all lighthouse keepers do this," Nat asked, "or is it just you?"

"Do what?"

"This." He gestured with his coffee cup to the storm and the ship. "Keep an all-night vigil with a shipwreck." He looked at her. "I think you'd do it even if your mother wasn't on board."

She nodded. Even Nat was calling her the keeper. She put her mug down on the rock. She *was* the keeper.

She listened to the wind and watched the ship rise with each wave that washed over the rocks. Her coffee was getting cold. Nat's head was down, and his breathing was quiet and even.

"What did you think of the house?" His voice came suddenly out of the darkness, and she jumped.

"The house?"

Nat nodded. "You know, my house." There was a pause. His eyes caught the faint light and twinkled. "You did look around, didn't you?"

Faith's cheeks burned. "It was . . . very nice," she said, stumbling over the words. "You keep it up very well."

Nat laughed. "I could see the lamplight moving from room to room," he admitted. "It's all right. I would have done the same thing if somebody else moved into my house."

"You haven't changed it much," Faith said. "I'm glad."
Nat said nothing.

"And it's so clean," Faith added, to fill up the awkward silence.

"You didn't expect it to be clean?" Nat put down his mug.

Faith blushed and was relieved he couldn't see her face very well. "I didn't think a man ... I mean ..." She sighed. "I just don't think of a man doing laundry and cleaning."

"Well, I don't think of a woman being a lighthouse keeper," he pointed out.

Faith had to laugh at that. "I guess not," she said.

Nat touched her arm. "You're always doing things people don't expect," he said. "I like that." He chuckled. "It's just hard to get used to."

Faith looked at him. "You're not as bad as I thought, either," she said, grinning.

Nat gave a shout of laughter. "See what I mean?" he said. "I think I'll take that as a compliment." He looked out at the ship. "We ought to tighten the line, don't you think?"

Faith nodded. She took hold of the rope, trying to ignore her stinging hands. It was easier to pull this time. "I think the wind's died down a bit," she said, noticing suddenly that the rain was lighter.

"Not enough yet," Nat said. They rewrapped the rope around the rock and rebuilt their tent. "It's going to be a long night."

And we don't know what will happen before morning, Faith added silently.

sixteen

Faith couldn't remember moving from the rock, but with the first light she woke to find herself curled in the sand with the oilcloth over her. Nat was nowhere to be seen.

She sprang up, heedless of her cold, stiff muscles. In the gray dawn light, she could see the *Mary* was listing heavily to the starboard side. She was still afloat, but Faith wondered if there would be anything left to salvage once the passengers were off.

"Hot coffee?" Nat came up behind her with a steaming mug and thrust it into her hands. "Better drink it quick, before it freezes." He smiled, but looked a bit grim all the same.

At his words, Faith became aware of the weather. It had stopped raining, but the wind was still high, and the sky was threatening. "It's blowing from the north, anyway," she said aloud. "Maybe it won't be a two-day storm after all."

Nat frowned. "It better not be. That schooner won't last another day." He gestured with his own mug to the *Mary*.

Even as they spoke, the ship jerked and slipped still more to starboard. Faith thought she heard a faint shout, and her heart seemed to jump into her throat. "We've got to get them off now," she said, taking a last gulp of the fast-cooling coffee. "Maybe they can rig up a bosun's chair." She stood up and took a look at the angle of the hawser connecting the ship to the rock. "It's too steep," she said, "and we shouldn't untie that, anyway. I wish they could float us another line."

Nat turned and scanned the cliffs behind them. "Where would we tie it?" he asked. "Can we get into one of those caves?"

In the dim morning light the small caves eroded into the bluff were little more than shadows. Faith considered it and shook her head. "It wouldn't work—they're too high up. We'd have to pull the bosun's chair uphill. But if we could lash the line to that tree"—she pointed to a strong sapling that seemed to be growing right out of the rock partway up the side of the cliff—"and the end on the ship was tied to the mast, it would work."

"Will the captain think of that?" Nat asked, peering out to the foundered vessel.

"If he's any good at all," Faith answered, "he'll already be floating us another line. See?" In the distance, they could see one of the sailors climbing the tallest mast, dragging a rope after him. Huge waves rocked the ship, and they could see him struggling upward, inch by inch. More than once he seemed to be flung into the wind like a rag doll; yet he kept hanging on to the rigging. Finally he stopped and appeared to be tying the line. On deck, Faith could see several other sailors grouped at the edge, waving a lit signal torch.

"They're floating in another line," Faith shouted. "It's going to be all right!"

She turned back to the cliff. "We need to get up to that tree with a line so we'll be ready."

Nat swallowed and rubbed his hands on his pants. "But it's straight up and nothing but rock. How can we get there?"

Faith thought he looked afraid. "I can do it," she said.

"I can get to the top of the cliff on Lady's trail and then lower myself over with rope. There's plenty in the boathouse." She started down the beach. "You watch for the line."

"No." Nat sounded angry. "I'll do the climbing." He put his hand out. "For pete's sake, Faith. I'm supposed to be the keeper. I can do something!" He managed a rueful grin. "*You* watch for the line." He took off at a run toward the boathouse to get some rope.

While she waited for Nat, Faith kept an eye on the ship. In the growing light, she could see figures moving on the deck, but she couldn't tell if her mother was one of them. "Please let her be all right," she whispered.

"Faith!" Nat shouted from the top of the cliff directly above her. She watched him tie a piece of rope around a huge old pine and test it for strength. Then, hanging another coil of rope over his shoulder, he grabbed the first piece with both hands. Bracing his feet, he lowered himself over the side of the cliff, heading for the narrow ledge where the young tree grew.

"Am I close?" He kicked out and looked down.

Faith made a small sound, but stopped herself from shouting. If he slipped now, she knew she could never break his fall. "You're right over the tree," she called up to him. "Just keep on coming straight down."

His feet touched the ledge, and then he was standing on it about twelve feet above her. "I'm ready," he said. He kept one end of the coiled rope over his shoulder and dropped the rest; it slithered to the bottom of the cliff. "Get the *Mary*'s line."

Faith waded into the water. She watched the ship rise and fall with each wave, knowing there was little time left. The schooner was taking an awful beating against the rocks.

"There!" she cried. In the morning light this life preserver was easier to spot, floating along on the tops of the waves. "I've got it!"

The life preserver had two lines attached. The other end of the thicker one was tied to the *Mary*'s mast. They would use the thinner line to haul the bosun's chair over the water to shore.

"Just hold on," she breathed, with one more glance to the schooner. "Only a few minutes more." She dragged the lines, still tied to the life preserver, back toward the cliff. She wrapped Nat's rope through the life preserver, over and over, back and forth, until she was sure it wouldn't get loose.

"What kind of a knot is that?" Nat said, looking down.

"One that holds," she called to him. "Just pull it up."

Nat pulled, and the life preserver with the ship's line attached began to rise into the air. Faith could hear him grunting with the effort.

Then he had it. He looped the line around the tree and dropped the life preserver back down to Faith. "Now pull," he commanded her. "We've got to get the line tight enough to hold a person."

Faith grabbed the rope and yanked as if she were pulling a giant bell rope. Faster and faster she pulled. When the rope was taut, she jumped up as high as she could, grabbed it, and hung there, letting her weight help tighten it even more.

"That's enough," Nat said at last. "Now untie the life preserver." Faith did that, and Nat pulled the end of the line up and tied it off. "I'm coming down."

"Do you think it'll hold?" Faith felt her stomach turn over. What if the rope broke when someone was coming across?

"It'll hold," Nat said. "You showed me how to tie the

knot, remember?" He grabbed the line and slid the rest of the way down until he was standing beside her on the beach. "Now," he said, looking out to the schooner, "let's hope they know what to do next."

In no time a bosun's chair was attached to the line by a pulley—suddenly the rope dipped low, and Faith could see a figure hanging underneath. Nat grabbed the light line, untied it from the life preserver, and quickly started hauling the sailor in the bosun's chair over the waves. Faith could see that one end of another line was attached to the chair—the other end was back on the *Mary*.

As soon as he reached the shore, the sailor jumped to the sand. Without his weight to hold it, the rope with the chair attached snapped high out of reach. When the sailors on the *Mary* saw the empty chair, they began hauling it back to the ship for another passenger.

The first sailor turned to Nat. "You did a fine thing, lad," he said. He held the line with one hand and grabbed Nat's arm with the other. "We'd be in a heap of trouble for sure if you hadn't been around." He nodded to Faith, looking at her curiously. "Your . . . ah . . . your sister, too," he added, clearing his throat.

Faith smiled at him and laughed to herself at his strange look. She knew she didn't look old enough to be a keeper's wife. But Nat certainly didn't look old enough to be her father, either. She caught Nat's eye, and they grinned at each other.

"How many people on board?" Faith asked him.

"Four passengers and the crew," he said. "We were carrying a load of lumber, but it washed off in the storm, along with all our belongings. There are two women on board; we'll get them off first. You'll have a full house tonight, miss." He looked at Nat and back to Faith, and she could imagine he was wondering where their parents were.

Before he could ask, a shout came from the ship, and the sailor began pulling on the line with all his might. When the bosun's chair got closer, Faith could see that a woman was the rider, and she suddenly felt as though she couldn't breathe. It was her mother.

She was pale, and Faith could see her hands shaking as she clung to the rope, but she was safe. Faith suddenly felt as light as a gull's feather. She wanted to run to her. She took a step forward, and then remembered her trousers and jacket. Her mother managed to look almost elegant even coming off a shipwreck. Faith pressed herself back against the cliff face and wished she was invisible.

The sailor helped her mother down from the chair, and when her feet touched the ground she clutched the man's arms. "Hurry," Faith's mother said, her voice trembling. "She'll go down in a minute. Please hurry."

"Yes, ma'am," the sailor said, playing out the line as the chair was whisked back to the ship for the next passenger. "We'll all get off. Never fear."

Faith's mother kept her eyes glued to the *Mary* and the bosun's chair coming slowly across the water carrying the other woman. She didn't even seem to see Nat, and she certainly didn't see Faith.

The other woman collapsed sobbing onto the sand when the sailor helped her off the chair. Faith's mother stooped down and put her arm around the woman's shoulders. "Stand up, Amelia," she said. "You'll catch your death of cold here. It will be warmer in the kitchen, and I'll get you a cup of tea."

She turned around. "Mr. Kent, would you be so kind . . ." Her voice trailed off as she caught sight of Faith.

Faith suddenly felt colder than she ever had when she was out battling the storm. She stood against the cliff, unable to move.

Her mother let go of the woman and walked toward Faith. "What are you doing here?" she asked. "And where on earth did you get those clothes?"

Faith was afraid to look at her mother's face. "I came to help the keeper," she said.

Her mother touched her arm gently, as though she couldn't believe Faith was real. "And to think I was thanking the Lord you were safe in Token Creek and not trying to help rescue this unlucky ship," her mother said. She put her hands on Faith's shoulders.

"Please don't be angry, Mama," Faith said. "I know I promised, but I just had to come." She swiped at her face with the soaking sleeve of her jacket, but the tears insisted on running down her cheeks.

A shout from the sailor interrupted her. "She's going down!" he cried. He was frantically hauling on the rope attached to the bosun's chair. Three men were riding it, and the chair sank closer and closer to the wild waves as the *Mary* slowly rolled over.

Faith ducked from her mother's hug and ran to help Nat and the sailor. She tried to put out of her mind the fact that her mother was watching every move she made.

The sailors left on the *Mary* jumped into the churning waves as the ship rolled. "Don't let go of that rope," Faith shouted to Nat and the sailor. "If they can grab it, they can pull themselves to shore."

She turned to see that the tree to which Nat had tied the line for the bosun's chair was bent almost double, and she knew it wouldn't hold much longer. While Nat and the sailor dragged the three men on the bosun's chair to safety, Faith grabbed that line. She knew she could never hold it herself, but if she could get it wrapped around the rock along with the hawser . . .

With a crack, the young tree snapped, and the line went

slack. Faith was ready. Before the weight of the sinking ship could put too much pressure on it, she had dragged it back to the rock. She got it wrapped only once around before it tightened, but that was enough, at least for the moment. Now there were two lifelines leading from the schooner to the beach, the hawser and the bosun's chair rope.

She looked up to see two sailors running toward her. "We can help you hold that, miss," one said. He was dripping wet; Faith figured he was one of the men clinging to the bosun's chair. He took the line from her hands, and he and his mate tied the heavy rope in a complicated knot around the rock.

Faith backed out of their way and looked up; Nat and one of the passengers were carrying a third man from the water. The man's feet dragged in the shallows, and his head hung down.

For a terrible instant Faith stood paralyzed as images of the last shipwreck washed over her. She watched as they laid the man gently on the sand. She could see by his clothes that he was one of the passengers, and when she saw her mother running, she knew it must be Mr. Chesterfield.

Faith clamped her hand over her mouth to keep from crying out. It couldn't be happening again. Her mother couldn't stand it. As she watched her mother kneel down beside the still body, all Faith's anger at the man didn't make any difference. She didn't know what she was going to do, but she *wasn't* going to let Mr. Chesterfield die.

seventeen

Faith turned and called to one of the sailors by the rock. "There's a barrel by the oil shed next to the lighthouse," she shouted. "An empty one. Go get it, quick."

The sailor glanced at the man on the beach and seemed to understand in a flash what was needed. "Yes, miss," he said, and ran off toward the lighthouse.

Faith raced to the unconscious Mr. Chesterfield. "Stay back," she said. "Give him some room."

Her mother, white as death herself, did as Faith told her. Faith knelt on the sand beside Nat, who was undoing Mr. Chesterfield's shirt buttons. "Is he breathing?" she asked him.

"I can't tell," Nat answered, his voice trembling. He bent over and rested his ear on his uncle's chest. "I don't think so."

The man's eyes were closed. His face was pale, and he had uncommonly long, dark lashes. He looked almost like a sleeping child. Like Willy, Faith thought, touching his cool cheek with her fingers. Her hands were shaking. She'd wished him out of their lives, but not like this.

She stroked his forehead, trying to imagine what her father would have done. Keep him warm? "Nat," she said, without looking away from Mr. Chesterfield's face, "get the oilcloth, and see what's taking them so long with the barrel."

Nat turned. "Here they come," he said, going for the oil-cloth.

Two sailors rolled the barrel up beside them. Faith stood up. "Can you lift him?" she asked them.

They already seemed to know what to do. One sailor put his hands under Mr. Chesterfield's arms, and the other grabbed his feet. Quickly they lifted him up, and Faith guided them to the barrel.

"Now drape him down over it," she said, holding the barrel to keep it from rolling. Mr. Chesterfield's head hung down over one side, and his feet dragged in the sand over the other side. "Get his head lower," she said. "We've got to let the water drain out of his lungs."

The sailors obeyed her without a word. She could hear her mother crying softly, and out of the corner of her eye she saw Nat holding the oilcloth.

Faith put her hand on Mr. Chesterfield's back. He was so still, and she wanted to scream for him to wake up. "Please," she murmured. "Please don't die."

She tried to remember what her father would do. She pushed gently on Mr. Chesterfield's back with one hand, and then two hands.

One of the sailors was squatting down by his head. "Water's coming out of his mouth," he said. "Do that again."

The other sailor steadied the barrel, and Faith pushed again, harder this time.

All of a sudden she felt Mr. Chesterfield's body jerk. He gasped and choked.

"Again!" the sailor shouted. Faith's mother cried out something, but Faith couldn't tell what.

Mr. Chesterfield started coughing, and vomited out an enormous amount of liquid. He coughed, choked, and vomited again.

"Now get him up," Faith cried. "Before he chokes to

death!"

The sailors grabbed Mr. Chesterfield's arms and dragged him off the barrel. They set him down in the sand, and turned him over so that he was half sitting half leaning against one sailor's leg.

"That's the way, sir," the sailor said as Mr. Chesterfield vomited a third time. He pounded him on the back.

Mr. Chesterfield coughed again. He took a giant breath, coughed once more, and then opened his eyes. "What's happening?" he said, frowning up at Faith, who was leaning over him. "What the devil are you doing here?"

Faith stared at him for a moment. Then she stood up straight and smiled at her mother. "I think he's going to be all right," she said, and stepped aside.

Her mother came quickly and knelt beside him. He was struggling to sit up. "Don't try to move," her mother said. "Just lie down."

"I won't lie down," Mr. Chesterfield said. "Let me go, man." He jerked away from the sailor's grasp.

"You almost drowned, sir," the sailor said, moving his hand away. "You ought to keep still."

Mr. Chesterfield grabbed hold of the sailor's shoulder and pushed himself to his feet. Then he reached a hand to Faith's mother and helped her up. The color had come back into her mother's cheeks, and Faith saw that she touched his arm lightly with her fingertips, as if reassuring herself that he was really there. Faith bit her lip. Her mother would never live at the lighthouse again, she thought. That much was clear.

"I want to know what you're doing here, Faith." Mr. Chesterfield's voice was husky, but loud enough.

Faith jumped. She closed her eyes, trying to think of an appropriate answer. For once she didn't want to start another argument.

"She was saving your life."

It was her mother's voice. Faith's eyes snapped open. This time the angry line of her mother's mouth was directed at Mr. Chesterfield.

"This is no place for a woman," he was insisting, but Faith's mother's hand on his wet jacket stopped him.

"You wouldn't say that if you'd seen her working." She turned to Faith. "Your father would have been proud of you." Her voice broke. Her eyes were bright, and suddenly she burst into tears.

"Mama . . . don't," Faith whispered, with tears running down her own cheeks. "Everything's fine." She wrapped her arms around her mother and saw how small she was. It felt like it had been years since she had hugged her. Faith didn't want to let go, ever. But she had to.

She watched as her mother murmured something to Mr. Chesterfield. Though the storm was receding, the waves still pounded the beach like drums, drowning out her words. They began to move away from the others. Faith's mother glanced back once, but Faith waved her on. "He needs to get inside where it's warm," she called.

"You did a mighty good deed, miss." One of the sailors nodded to her. "He should have thanked you."

Faith shook her head. "He's still feeling poorly," she said. She wasn't sure at all that he'd thank her, now or ever. But, somehow, that didn't matter anymore.

Faith watched them. Mr. Chesterfield walked on unsteady legs and he leaned heavily on her mother's shoulder. She stopped herself from going to help. There was no need. Her mother's steps were strong and steady as she led him to the house.

Nat was busy coiling up the rope and, from the back, in the blue keeper's uniform, he looked like her father. The resemblance startled her.

KEEPER OF THE LIGHT

"Faith!" He motioned her over and handed her a prickly circle of rope. "Can you help me with this?" he said.

"Of course." She hooked the coil over her shoulder. Nat took the other one, and they walked together to the boathouse.

Lady was standing patiently, eyes closed. She seemed to have fully recovered from the ride to the lighthouse; she looked as contented as if she was at home in her stall. Her water bucket was empty, and while Faith hung the rope coils on their hooks, Nat led Lady down to the lake for a drink.

Faith stood alone in the dim boathouse. One end of the lifeboat was still suspended from the rafters by rope; the end she'd managed to untie when she was going to launch it lay in the dirt. It was a new lifeboat; it had never been used except in drills. She ran her hand along the gunwale, savoring the smooth feel of sanded wood and new paint. It had almost been used, she thought. If she'd been here alone she would have taken the lifeboat out. She would have drowned. Like her father.

For the first time, the thought came without pain. Perhaps her father had made a mistake that night. She mulled that idea over for a moment. Maybe she'd learned something from Nat after all. Maybe she'd be an even better keeper than her father because of it. She grabbed hold of the rope, still hanging from the rafter, tied it to the lifeboat, and was hauling it up when Nat and Lady came back.

"You've still got a lot to teach me," Nat said, helping her pull on the rope until the lifeboat hung properly suspended once more. "Do you think I'll ever know as much about keeping the light as you do?"

"I hope not," Faith said, laughing at him. "I'm after your job, you know."

He nodded. "I figured as much," he said, eyes twinkling. "But my uncle would never hire a woman. I think I'm safe."

"Don't be too sure of that. My mother seems to have a lot of influence over your uncle, don't you think?"

Nat grinned. "You may be right," he said. He opened the boathouse door with a flourish and tipped his hat as Faith walked out ahead of him. The sky was still gray, but getting lighter. There was a fire in the stove; Faith could see the smoke swirling in the wind. And beyond that, the lighthouse waited.

Bibliography

The following books have historical information on and stunning photographs of lighthouses on the Great Lakes:

Hyde, Charles K. *The Northern Lights: Lighthouses of the Upper Great Lakes.* Color photographs by Ann and John Mahan. Lansing, MI: TwoPeninsula Press, 1986.

Roberts, Bruce, and Ray Jones. *Great Lakes Lighthouses.* Old Saybrook, CT: The Globe Pequot Press, 1994.

For more information on women lighthouse keepers, see:

Clifford, Mary Louise, and J. Candace Clifford. *Women Who Kept the Lights: An Illustrated History of Female Lighthouse Keepers.* Williamsburg, VA: Cypress Communications, 1993.

The shore of Lake Superior near Munising is known as "The Graveyard" because of the large number of ships that have wrecked on its rocky coastline. For more information, see:

Stonehouse, Frederick. *Munising Shipwrecks.* Au Train, MI: Avery Color Studios, 1983.